DEMONS, INK

CLAYTON SNYDER

ROGUE PUBLISHING

First Edition
First Edition: February 2021

❀ Created with Vellum

For those who try to do the right thing, even if they fuck it up.
There are few things more human.

1

"Thomas Edison once said: *Non-violence leads to the highest ethics, which is the goal of all evolution. Until we stop harming all other living beings, we are still savages.* Two problems there. One: ol' Tom never faced down a biker with a knife. Two: that motherfucker electrocuted an elephant to prove a point, so you'll forgive me if I assume he's full of shit. Violence is a red thread in a white sheet, a bloody streak coloring everything we do.

"But really, this is just academic twaddle when you're punching a guy in the face. You have to understand, it's not personal. People hire me to do things, and I do them."

The man grunted as my fist connected and knocked a tooth out. I hammered my knuckles into the guy's face again, and he crumpled. A growl escaped me. Inside, Regnos still wanted to hit him, and I clenched, forcing the demon back. She snarled once, and let it go.

The biker groaned, blood spilling from a cut on his forehead onto the pavement. I knelt and pulled the wallet from his back pocket, rifling through the contents until I found the dollar I'd been looking for.

I mean, it was a special dollar. I'm not a lunatic.

———

The cab bumped and shook with every pothole, and still I fought off sleep. The demons took a lot out of me, and though the tattoos kept them in check for the most part, they still had enough juice to sap my energy. I can't say when they showed up. Maybe they'd been with me since birth, maybe they'd come around when they heard me crying at night, alone in the dark.

Whatever the reason, they were here. I spent a lot of years fighting them, denying them, and generally self-destructing. I spent a lot of time in and out of trouble. Later, I met a man who taught me their language, and how to bind them. I owed the man my life, but for reasons only the universe knows, he's dead now, and I'm alone again. Sometimes it rains, sometimes the world substitutes the rain for shit.

The cab hit another massive pothole, jouncing me up against the felt-covered ceiling for a second, making my skull ache. I gritted my teeth as the cabbie slammed on the brakes, sending me careening into the divider.

"How much, Evel Knievel?" I asked after I finished picking threads of red upholstery from my incisors.

He gave me the price and I tossed him a little extra, because while the ride sucked, I don't cheap on tips. The cab pulled away, the tires splashing as the clouds overhead started to weep. The blue neon out front of the building read 'THE STONE', the light throwing the street into garish shades.

Not the sort of place you'd catch someone who could afford to not be there. And still, it was a bit high-class for my taste. I preferred to drink with people who made their money honestly. Still, my employer owned the place, so I had little choice. I stepped inside, warmth pushing away the chill from the rain.

The sound of the blues and the sharp tang of alcohol greeted me, and I pushed past small tables filled with nuzzling couples and across tasteful carpet to a walnut and brass bar. A man roughly the size of a small mountain eyeballed me.

I'll admit to a certain amount of cynicism in regards to men with more muscle mass than neck. I suspect most rent their brains on a time-share. If Rizzo was any indication, he only got it every third weekend. Still, I did my best not to underestimate someone who could bench-press a Buick. I shot him a friendly nod.

"Hey Rizzo," I said.

"Hey Jack."

"Boss in?"

He reached under the table and I tensed. If Rizzo or his boss, Vincent, suddenly decided to give me a pink slip, it was coming in the form of a shotgun shell. Instead, his hand lingered for a second then withdrew. I breathed the sort of sigh announcing your bowels have decided not to decorate your pants. There are few things in my line of work to make a man tense and threaten to fill his shorts with pudding like a hand disappearing for even the briefest of moments.

I'd seen a lot of violence. Done my fair share of it. And I knew it only took a few seconds to do a fair share of damage. Fighting and killing ain't like you see in movies. Fights are short and brutal, a lot of close-in work depending on how many times you can bounce the other guy's brain against the inside of his skull or starve it of oxygen. Sometimes a hand goes into a coat, or under a counter, and comes back with a knife, or a gun, or a club. People take wounds, and are haunted by them for weeks, months at a time. If they survive.

Sometimes they do the opposite. Then some poor flatfoot from uptown has to chalk around your body and lay evidence cards when he'd rather be eating takeout in his squad car. A whole host of uniforms take pictures, dig under your nails, and tell your mother you're expired meat. If they find you, anyway.

It's the sort of thing capable of making a man nervous down to his dangly bits.

A small man with a thick nose and wide-set eyes entered through a door behind the bar, breaking up my thoughts. He the sort of expensive suit that probably cost more than the sum of my entire life's pay, and the air of a man used to being listened to. More than listened to—obeyed. In another life, he might've been the world's worst middle manager. As it was, he only a step above.

Vincent Cagliostro. Businessman. Weasel. Thug. He'd come into his empire the old-fashioned way, by making it clear to his rivals he was intolerant of competition. Volatile at the best of times, but with an eye for talent, and deep pockets. Part of me was sure he had more than deep pockets and a good nose. He'd been operating pretty much in the open for years, and I suspected he had a patron behind the scenes.

I skipped the pleasantries and tossed the dollar on the counter, a speck of blood vibrant against the green. Vince picked it up and tucked it away.

"Thanks," he said and passed a brown envelope across the bar.

I took it and tucked it into my jacket. I didn't count it. I'm not suicidal.

"What's with the dollar?" I asked.

The smart part of me winced and cursed internally. Questions were the sort of thing that caught a guy nicknames like Freddy Nine Fingers and Joe Who Ain't Alive No More. Heaven is filled with cats and contractors who had to ask *why*.

Vince eyed me for a moment. "It's cursed."

He watched me, waiting for a reaction. I didn't give him one. I had bound demons to myself and had seen stranger shit still. Besides, I was in the business of doing violence, not asking questions which might see me floating in the river.

"Interesting," I said.

"Yeah," he turned and left the way he'd come, leaving me to stand awkwardly with Rizzo.

"Uh… I'll be going now," I said.

Rizzo did his best impression of a wall and ignored me.

———

The ride home was smoother than the ride to The Stone, and I thought maybe the cabbie was my reward for a rough night. I exited the cab with a bigger tip than the last since I was feeling flush, and climbed the stairs to my apartment. I tossed my keys on the table and kicked the door shut. Cory's glow lit the studio. I entered the kitchen, popping open the fridge and fishing out a beer. Cory swirled in his jar, a disembodied soul agitated about something. I took a sip, letting the alcohol wash the aches of the day off.

"Where you been, man?" Cory asked.

"Workin'."

I wanted to be annoyed with him, with his neediness, but it was hard. Looking at him swirling around the Mason jar—you can imagine how lonely it got. Besides, Cory and I had a complicated relationship. We were lovers, once. Then he killed Ramirez, and I paid a witch by the name of Ivy to trap his soul in a jar. I'm still not sure why he did it, or if he even feels bad about it.

"You can't tell me? Fine. Fuck you," he wheedled.

"Fuck you too, buddy," I replied.

A sullen silence followed while the things we'd never said hung in the air. I finished my beer and left it on the table, then crawled into bed.

———

I'm drowning. But before, I'm walking, feet on the rocks, water cold against my shins. I'm what, seven? Eight? My grandparents on the shore, and my grandfather, tall and lean in the summer sun, calls out.

"Not too far. There's a drop-off."

But the water is clear. I can look down and see the bottom. It's called Crystal Lake for a reason. I step out, and the water rises, but my feet are still firm, the chill in the water taking my breath for a moment.

"Not too far!"

I look back and wave and step, another step, then a step to adjust against an incoming wave. The bottom goes out, like someone forgot to finish the bed beneath. The world goes dark, and I'm breathing water, but you can't breathe water, you ain't got gills, silly wabbit. I thrash and try to scream, and my breath struggles to come, but I'm holding my mouth shut, keeping the lake out, because if I don't, every ounce of water will try to force its way into my guts and lungs, and that will be it.

Pressure squeezes me, my vision blots and spots and threatens to go back. I inhale despite my own warnings, and cold water rushes in. I sputter and choke, but the waves are a blanket over my head, and no one hears.

And then, thrashing and sinking, and sinking, a hand, strong and tan and weathered pulls me up like I'm made of driftwood.

I cling to the owner—my grandfather—smelling of sun and tobacco and aftershave, and I'm crying, but it's okay because today isn't the day I die.

———

I woke in the small hours, weeping. A voice, Cory's, called from the other room.

"Jack?"

I didn't reply, memory hammering into me like time has fists, and it meant to teach me a lesson. I laid awake until the small hours, regret filling up the minutes between. It was some time before I slept again.

When someone wants to hire me, one of two things happen. Either I get a letter in a PO Box, or someone hammers on my door until I open it with a headache and an attitude. Why not get with the modern world? Because I like the sound of my own thoughts. TV, streaming, smart phones, little TVs at gas pumps, music piped into stores—there's never a moment alone.

If I were a paranoid man, I'd think someone didn't want us to have a moment to think about the state of the world. But it's a cynical thought, even for me. I want to believe the best of people. It's too bad they're more than willing to show us the worst.

When I woke up that morning, it was to the door shuddering in the frame, the fist on the other side threatening to shiver the wood to flinders. I stood and staggered toward the source. I felt like sleep was a foreign country, one with me on some sort of no-fly list. To top it off, my mouth tasted like I'd licked a cat.

"One sec!" I said.

I undid the lock and flung the door open. The blonde woman on the other side looked like she'd caught one eyebrow with a fishhook. She sniffed and strutted past me, peering first into the kitchen and the bathroom, then the living room, a simple space with a futon and a mural I'd painted on one wall. She gestured at the painting—flowering vines climbing the wall.

"That's nice. Your work?"

"I dabble," I said.

She looked at the futon and its crumpled bedsheets. My rational mind was berating me in a voice not unlike Martha Stewart's. I tamped it down mentally, locking it in a closet. In my defense, I hadn't even pissed yet. Llyrial stirred then, trying to push out waves of lust.

Now, I'm not a bad-looking guy. Tall, dark, a little rough around the edges. You wouldn't believe how much a broken nose and a few scars make a difference. But I'm still human, and like most humans, I only attract what I put out. That's where Llyrial comes in. If Regnos was the muscle, Llyrial was all pheromone and subtle suggestion—an almost hypnotic urge appealing to baser instinct, like drums just beyond hearing.

I squashed the demon's need, but saw the woman's reaction regardless—flushed cheeks, dilated pupils—and I coughed to break the spell.

"Can I help you?" I asked.

She shook herself—a small motion sending her shoulders and hips swaying, and I clamped down on the demon again before he found his rhythm. I sometimes wondered what the point of carrying around the embodiment of lust was, but figured I was never going to get an answer.

Some people wake up craving milk, some people stop what they're doing for a smoke. Me, I get the random urge to bed the closest person to me. Not all demons offer a mutual pact. Like the genie said: phenomenal cosmic power, *itty-bitty living* space. Besides, some things you just don't get to know.

She reached into her blazer and I tensed. If someone decided I knew too much, or had become a threat, this would be a good way to kill me. But I had safeguards. I'd had Ivy paint wards into the mural after I finished it—runes I could activate to immobilize unpleasant people, and despite the low-rent image the apartment threw off, it was defensible. As a last resort, I had a pistol under the bed, assuming I got to it before someone turned me into a Jackson Pollock painting.

I liked to see clients in person, sniff them out. I got the impression the woman standing in front of me was formidable, but safe for now, like a lioness viewed from afar. I relaxed a fraction and her hand came out, holding a business card. I took it, the paper crisp and white, thick. A name was embossed on the front: Mark Jacobs.

"That's nice, but who are you?" I asked.

"I'm Mr. Jacobs'… liaison."

"That's not a name."

She smiled in a way that could have frozen gasoline. So, she knew better. Names have power, and some of the less savory elements of the Umbra—the supernatural community—would be more than happy to show you to what extent.

"Fair enough," I said. "How can I help Mr. Jacobs?"

"Be at the address on the card by noon today."

She left, and I watched her go. I wanted to say I didn't take jobs without knowing more, but that was bullshit. I'd taken jobs on a whim. I'd taken jobs over a bet. I'd taken jobs when asked by a pretty woman, and this one certainly counted. The smarter part of me was ringing warning bells like Quasimodo on amphetamines. I told myself I'd listen. I probably lied.

———

After she left, I cleaned up and dug out the closest thing to respectable clothes I could find. I stood in the kitchen in a battered suit, something I'd bought with my last couple hundred dollars my first week out of prison. Back then, I'd believed though I'd been through Hell, the worst of it was behind me. I believed I'd paid my debt. The world would open itself to me like a flower, and I'd pluck the blossom with just a smile and a hard work ethic. Looking back, I realize I was full of shit. Prison is a brand burned so deep the bone still throbs.

Cory's spirit swam in blue ripples through the space of his jar.

"Big meeting?" he asked.

I adjusted my tie. "Tie or no tie?" I asked, ignoring the question.

"I always liked you without."

I pulled the tie away and glared at it, then tossed it on the table. Even when you're feuding with someone, if they're right, they're right. Half-dead, and still with impeccable taste. Mr. Blackwell would be so lucky.

9

"Relax," Cory said.

"I'd love to. At least this is a public meeting." The address on the card was an outdoor bistro on the west side.

Plenty of witnesses. Or at least I assumed no one would try to off me in place where they served burgers and beer. That sort of thing tends to put people off business for a while—yours and theirs. Hard to enjoy a double Slawsome with extra slaw when the guy at the table next to you is face-down in his fries.

"What're you so nervous about?" Cory asked.

"Well, I keep thinking about that one meeting—what, three years ago? You know, when no one showed up and you murdered Diego?"

"That's hurtful," Cory said, his voice subdued.

"How do you think I feel? You ready to tell me why you did it?"

"I keep telling you, I don't know. Don't you think I'd tell you, Jack? Don't you think I'd want to tell you?"

"I don't know what you'd do anymore."

Cory didn't reply, and I left, the sound of the slamming door punctuating my exit. I seethed on the other side for a minute. Some wounds never heal. They just scab over for a time.

Flamberge was a trendy restaurant sitting on the edge of the town square, a bit of the hipster creeping into a city so uptight if you shoved a piece of coal up its ass, it'd shit a diamond the next day. And then invest it. The whole place was open-air—tall round tables surrounded by barstools beside a smoking and sizzling brick grill, sending the scents of beef, asparagus, and eggplant across the plaza. I took a table and ordered a beer, something local and malty.

Mark Jacobs found me in short order, looking like clothing rack with a nerve problem. He was a tall thin black man in an expensive suit and a tic making the side of one eye jump like someone was sticking him with a needle. His eyes were red, and the suit hung on him like a sheet on a set of antlers. Grief was rarely a mask, and more often a shroud. And his was fresh. He settled beside me; voice pitched low.

"Are you Nyx?" he asked.

I nodded.

"It's fine," I said. "Part of doing what I do means no one knows what I actually do. You can speak up."

I hoped to calm him a little. He looked like a cat someone's just discovered in their attic. It's the sort of thing that attracts attention neither of us needed.

He cleared his throat, and when he spoke again, it was clearer, but the rasp remained. He seemed to me a man on the edge of a breakdown. I'd have to step lightly. Men in that mindset are brittle glass over a pit of razors. Push too hard, and they break and fall in. He fished inside his jacket, and I found myself involuntarily flinching. Maybe it was catching.

"My daughter," he said, and pushed a photo across the table to me.

I picked it up. The girl in the photo was about six or seven, cherubic, happy. She had her father's eyes and tiny braids. He took it back and smiled, a wan thing clinging to his lips like a life preserver on a drowning man.

"She's got her mother's smile," he said.

"What happened, Mr. Jacobs?"

"I had... debts."

"To men you don't want to owe, and they took her."

He looked at me, and his eyes could have broken my heart a hundred times. "I can't pay."

My stomach knotted. I saw where this was going. I either helped free a little girl, and pissed off some unpleasant people, or I refused, and became the monster I'd spent years trying to deny. For a moment, I wished I hadn't opened the door that morning.

Then I hated myself for the thought, and a wave a guilt washed over me. I'd had two fathers. My grandfather, and Ramirez. Some people are never so lucky. Just because I lost both didn't mean I had the right to deny this girl a chance to know hers.

I took the photo, gently, from Mark's hand.

"What do you know?" I asked.

Relief flooded his face. "They took her Tuesday. They gave me until Saturday."

Shit. It was already Wednesday at noon, and I was just getting started. I nodded like he hadn't just backed up a dump truck full of bad news and unloaded it on me.

"Do you know where?" I asked.

He shook his head. "No. Sorry."

"Do you know who?" I did my best to keep panic and irritation out of my voice.

"Caleb Cotton."

I frowned. I didn't know the guy, but maybe Ivy did, or could find out. I wondered if he was a new player. It seemed unlikely Vincent wouldn't have already heard of him, or that he hadn't sent Rizzo to explain the way the world worked. Crime lords are shockingly territorial, and kidnapping in Vincent's territory would have been as good as pissing on his door. My brain spun with possibilities. Still—I looked at the photo, at the little girl, and swallowed the butterflies.

"You'll have her back," I promised.

Mark practically collapsed on the table, clasping my hands in his. They were warm and a little damp. I held them for a moment anyway. He trembled, a small vibration running through his skin. I thought again of the price of loss.

"Thank you. Thank you," he said.

A waiter I hadn't seen cleared his throat beside me. I looked over.

"I told him I'm picking up the check," I said. The waiter rolled his eyes and walked away.

———

I'd decided to hoof it to Ivy's. Despite a promising start to the day, rain began on my walk over, and by the time I reached her neighborhood, the drizzle developed into a downpour. It fell in fat droplets hammering the pavement, sending ripples across puddles as they landed, shaking the little pools in shimmering rainbows skittering across the oily asphalt. Ivy's apartment was ten floors up in a loft she claimed was rent controlled, but I suspected the landlord had been hexed into submission. I mean, she's a good witch, not a perfect one.

I watched traffic pass from a doorway across the street, rubbing the tattoos on my arms absently. It wasn't that I was afraid. I was terrified. I tried to remind myself Ivy and I had been friends for a long time, but we hadn't spoke much since the Cory incident. I'd watched the woman pull the soul out of a living body and stuff it into a jar with all the professional detachment of a chef canning beets. That sort of thing tends to give a guy pause. Makes you think of the little things, you know? Chocolate. Sex. Not having your spirit trapped in a space smaller than an uptown studio.

"Whatcha doin?"

The voice at my elbow caused me to jump roughly a foot in the air, a high-pitched squeak escaping my throat, the sound like a strangled cat. Her laughter followed, deep and melodic. I turned, my hands shaking a little, and came face to face with Ivy. A grin split her face, and her eyes danced mischief.

"Jesus, Ivy," I said.

She laughed again, and I marveled at how a six-foot woman managed to sneak up on me. A man passing by gave us both side-eye and stepped across the street, his step hurried. The smile dropped from Ivy's face. I internally uh-ohed.

"IS IT BECAUSE I'M BLACK?" she shouted at his retreating

back, then gave me a smirk, hand on hip. "Goddamn white people. Present company excluded, of course," she said.

"And Tom Hiddleston," I reminded her.

She arched an eyebrow and pointed with one perfectly manicured finger. "Loki to you."

And like that, the tension in my shoulders melted. I had built Ivy into this scary-ass witch over the past year and forgot what a delightful person she was. That's the problem with time and distance. It lies like a man caught in a whorehouse. She hugged me, then pulled back and gave me a once-over.

"You look like someone fed you a shit sandwich. C'mon, let's get out of the rain," she said, tugging on my arm.

She led me to her building, and I followed her up to a penthouse on the tenth floor. When she opened the door, I stood for a moment, taking it in. When some people think 'witch', they think a hut deep in the forest, a cauldron, maybe a wart. Instead, Ivy's place was decorated in a kitschy art déco modern blend that somehow worked. Pristine movie posters in frames hung on the walls, everything from Lady Hawke to Black Panther, alongside black and white prints of the city, and shelves of books.

I liked Ivy's place. The smell reminded me of my mother's baking, the way she'd lay cookies out on the rustling paper, the way the melted lard would stain the brown sheets in spreading rings. But not in a creepy way. It was a homey smell. Not an Oedipal one.

The scent would permeate the house, brown sugar and chocolate blending together, sweet and thick, the way I imagined the witch's house from Hansel and Gretel would have smelled. I thought of that smell on crisp autumn mornings, on cold winter afternoons, and the way the sun shone against the white housecoat my mother wore when the chill crept into the house like a thief, stealing warmth from the tips of our fingers and toes.

To top it off, Ivy was completely wartless. If I wasn't such a gormless bastard, I'd suggest she was beautiful, but never to her face. I still had a healthy respect for not being turned into a newt. Besides, the wound from Cory's betrayal still felt raw some days. I was attracted to her, but not enough to make a move yet. Or maybe that was self-preservation. Libido and heart don't always mix, and my libido was chained to a demon. Like a peanut butter cup, except the peanut butter is also packed with heroin.

She flopped down onto a white leather couch and raised an eyebrow at me.

"Doors keep the air in better when they're closed. And stop gawping. You look like a gomer."

I closed the door and took an overstuffed recliner across from her, its white leather cool and soft. She let me settle in, and then leaned forward, elbows on knees.

"Been a long time, Jack."

"Yeah, sorry. I was…"

"Avoiding me?"

"It sounds so rude when you put it that way."

She nodded. "No, I get it. I put your boyfriend in a jar."

"Yeah, that can be unsettling."

Silence fell between us for a minute. I pretended to inspect a foot-tall statue of Loki. Accurate down to his codpiece.

"So, what happened?" she asked, snapping my attention back.

"Why am I here, you mean?"

"Yeah."

I sighed. "Someone took a kid."

She let out a low breath. "Well, shit."

I nodded.

Her eyebrow shot back up. "No quips? You must be serious."

"I don't know the guy who supposedly took her. Never heard of him, and if he's operating in this town, and hasn't been capped yet, he's either an unknown, or a scary bastard," I said. "On top of it, I've got less than three days to find her."

"Or what?"

I shrugged. "No idea. I figured you might be able to drum up a lead," I said. "But…"

"But what?"

"I'm worried about what might happen if I get you involved."

"Thanks. Save your overprotective bullshit for someone who can't turn a guy into a puddle of goo. Got more wards laid on this place than a Suicide Girl's got tattoos."

"Your knowledge of porn never ceases to amaze me."

It was her turn to shrug. "Girl's got to have a hobby. You really worried about this?"

"I mean, if this was a punching situation, Regnos could just tear them to shreds."

She stood and wandered to the kitchen. I heard the clink of ice, the slosh of liquid, then something rattling, like metal on glass. When she returned, it was with a glass of whiskey, and a Mason jar filled with coins. She handed me the jar, kept the whiskey for herself. I held up the coins.

"What's this for laundry day?" I asked.

She gave me a look that said if I were any dumber, she'd have to start putting corks on my forks. "A jar of coins."

"Ha. Ha. Haaaa," I mocked, and spun the lid off. I reached inside, pulling one out.

A patina of age clung to the silver. One side held a number of symbols I didn't recognize, the other an hourglass. The metal felt like it carried a faint charge. I frowned.

"Talismans?" I asked.

She nodded around the glass. "Yeah, I make them for the high anxiety clients off the street. They don't really need them, but it makes them feel better."

"So, they're fake?"

Ivy made a face. "How dare you," she said in mock outrage. "I am an honorable witch. Even if they don't need them, the world is a fucked-up place."

I stuffed one in my pocket, and my anxiety dropped a little, the relief like when your ears pop after a plane descends.

"Thanks," I said. "What's it for?"

She let go a long-suffering sigh, like I couldn't possibly be this obtuse. "If he's a heavy hitter, he's gonna have a little mojo backing him up. Can you deflect curses?"

"I once stopped a bowling ball with my face."

"That *does* explain some things."

"HA HA," I said, as loud and obnoxiously as possible. "So, about that lead…"

"Ah. Ah." She wagged a well-manicured finger at me.

"What?" I tried to look innocent.

Ivy held up a finger and a thumb, rubbing them together. I sighed and dug a crumpled twenty from another pocket.

"Mercenary," I said.

"Pragmatist," she corrected.

I shrugged and set the rest of the jar down. "Now what?"

She sipped the whiskey. The room fell silent. I could almost hear the wheels spinning as she worked her big brain over.

"I might know a guy," she said.

"What kind of guy?" I asked, the anxiety trying to worm its way back in.

She waved a hand, ice clinking, whiskey sloshing. "A guy. You know."

"I feel like you're hedging."

"No."

"He's a witch, isn't he?"

She took a long sip of whiskey.

"Ivy?" I persisted.

"Well, technically, warlock."

"God damn it." My stomach did a flip, and even the demons raised a little hell in my head. None of us were fond of soul brokers, despite the relationship we had with Ivy.

Witches and warlocks were as close to the top of human food

chain as you could get. Witches, then demonites, humans, lawyers, and finally politicians. If we were the AK-47 of magic, witches were the nukes. Granted, I knew my fair share of extras, again, thanks to Ivy and the things under my skin, but I was still considered a middling talent. Only the Enclave approached the level of scary pure magicians could conjure.

"What can he do that you can't?" I asked.

"He finds things. Never was my specialty."

"What's it gonna cost me?"

"Depends on if he likes you."

"So, a lot?"

She shrugged. "Maybe. But I adore you, so I'll put in a good word."

"Got a name?"

"Sebastian Locke."

"Really?"

She nodded. "Witchin' ain't easy. You think Ivy Sosye is my real name?"

I blinked. It had never occurred to me. "I. Uh…"

She laughed. "Dumb and ugly. Poor thing."

"What *is* your name?" I asked, curiosity tickling my brain.

"Like I'm telling you." She emptied her glass. "Okay, hun. You need to get your pasty ass out of my house. Girl's gotta hustle," she said.

"But…" I wheedled.

"Keep that talisman on you. You'll be fine."

"And if I'm not?"

She shrugged. "You will be."

We stood, and she walked me out. We didn't hug at the door or shake hands. Just a quick goodbye. Ivy slipped me a card with Locke's address on it, and then the door closed, leaving me in a quiet hallway.

———

N ot all members of the Umbra make Ivy-stacks of money. Some are natural entrepreneurs, others predators. And some are junkies. They like the power too much to spend time turning it into anything, instead choosing to tap in at every opportunity. And some simply didn't have the power. Ivy tried explaining it to me once, in terms of gas tanks. Some people are sixteen-wheelers, and some are Fieros.

The address on the card led to an alley behind a Starbucks. The smell of roasted beans and garbage hung in the air, pressed tight between the buildings. A trio of men leaned against one wall, shirtsleeves rolled up to their shoulders, backpacks sitting beside them. The smell of cigarette smoke joined the food, the three of them looking up when I entered.

"Mr. Locke?" I asked.

Ivy hadn't given me a description, just an address and a coin. I had the feeling she liked to fuck with me at times. *See Jack squirm. Squirm Jack, squirm.* A skinny man with dusky skin and ink on his wrists held my gaze at the question. I couldn't see what was there, but a part of my gut twisted. I pushed it away and focused on the task at hand.

"Sorry, Ivy sent me," I said.

He nodded and said something to the other men, who laughed for a moment, one reaching out to pat him on the back as he passed. He approached with a grin still clinging to his lips from the conversation. Regnos was convinced he'd called me a pencil dick. I ignored her.

"How can I help you?" he asked.

"Ivy mentioned you were good at finding things."

"Depends. I don't do car keys or pets."

I shook my head. "I have a more… concrete problem."

He noticed the tattoos crawling up my arms for the first time. "I suppose you do. Please, continue."

"There's a missing girl."

Locke nodded. "Got anything that belonged to her?"

I shook my head. "Uh, no."

"Fine. I'll need a little blood."

I squirmed a little inside, as predicted. The last thing I wanted was a warlock having a piece of me, but it seemed I had little choice. I didn't like my odds when it came to Cotton. He was an unknown quantity, and something still felt off, like a gate with a squeaky hinge. This put us on common ground at least. Well, close. I mean, he could have a bazooka.

I held out my hand, and Locke produced a bowl from his backpack, the inside caked with a red substance leaving little to the imagination. He stabbed my index finger with a pin, quick and almost painless. Blood welled from the wound, dripping into the bowl, and Locke motioned for me to move back.

He dropped the pin in and lit a match. The flame guttered for a moment before steadying, then he dropped it in as well. The match sizzled, and a thin wisp of smoke rose. It formed a shape I couldn't quite make out but seemed to make sense to Locke. He nodded and waved a hand, breaking up the fumes, then looked up at me.

"Payment?" he asked.

"How much?"

"A favor."

The bottom dropped out of my stomach. My mother used to say a favor owed is a burden given, she'd been right about one thing, at least. I nodded despite myself.

"What is it?" I asked.

"Hold onto this." He handed me a dollar, faded. The paper was thin and wrinkled—it'd been around.

"What am I supposed to do with this?" I asked.

"When the time comes, you'll know."

"Great."

He smiled. I shrugged and dropped it into my pocket. Probably a witch thing.

"Okay, where is she?" I asked.

"No idea."

"What?" I asked, my voice rising like a man who's just caught his balls in his zipper. Locke's friends looked over and snickered. He held up a hand. "I know where she will be, though."

"Okay, where?" My capacity for patience had taken a precipitous dive.

"Warehouse in the south side. Kruger Industries. Tomorrow morning."

I looked at him a little longer, trying to determine if this was just a con, but he'd already lost interest in me, turning back to his friends. He said something in a language I didn't understand and rejoined them to the sound of laughter. I wandered from the alley, the dollar brushing against my thigh through the thin fabric of my pocket, a reminder I didn't know what the fuck I was doing.

2

I t's 1980… something. Sunday, I know that much. The old man sits in his La-Z-Boy, its overstuffed upholstery holding his beer-soaked form tight. The TV is blaring, little men in uniforms jostling for a ball, Pat Summerall's voice like warm honey over the tinny roar of the crowd from the speakers. A forty nestles in his hand, dew from the late summer heat coalescing in a little pool of the web where thumb meets palm. The whistles blow, and he curses at a play on the screen, the referee tossing a flag and waving his arms.

My head is resting on the arm of the chair, and I ask a question—what was that, what's an offside, maybe what's a first down. I am eight. Without a word, his free hand draws back like a piston and his fist hammers into the spot where my scalp meets my forehead. I see stars and topple back, tears springing to my eyes. I feel blood, hot and wet, trickling down my forehead, and I'm crying.

He barely sees what he did, staggering to the bathroom and running hot water. He throws a washcloth at me and tells me to hold it on the cut. To stop crying, I'm not dead. I suck the sniffles in and hold the cloth to the throbbing ache in my skull.

Eventually, it stops bleeding, and he tells me to wash the cloth out. The game plays in the background, the beer still in his hand, the men *fighting over a ball for millions of dollars, and pain behind my eyes. I stand at the sink and watch the pink run out of the white cloth, wring it out again and again, hoping I don't miss any, because that would lead to an explanation, would lead to more pain.*

When I'm done, I climb the stairs to my room and lie in the dark, hot tears streaming from my eyes, soaking my pillowcase. Sobs threaten to tear from my chest, and I stifle them, rage instead growing, growing...

————

I woke, my face hot and wet, my knuckles bruised and bleeding. I'd hammered a hole in the drywall above the futon. Red tinted the drywall pink. Regnos raged in my chest, an angry renter in a shitty apartment, promising to burn it to the ground if someone doesn't fix the heat.

I seized on the picture of Gabriel, my ex-flame, beside the bed. She stood in sunlight beside bright water, smiling. Regnos grabbed it. With a grunt, I hammered it deep into the drywall, the frame splintering, glass shattering. Blood flowed from my palm, and I slapped my hand against Regnos' tattoo with a shout.

The demon receded into the background, rage trickling from me. The slap left a bloody handprint on my chest. I ripped a strip off my sheet and wrapped it around my hand, staunching the flow from the worst of the wounds.

It wasn't that I wanted to hurt anyone, I just wanted to break something. Sometimes rage needs an outlet, and in the case of Regnos, sometimes she has to bleed something to be sated. I stared at the picture of Gabriel for another minute, then took a deep breath.

There was a rabbit hole I didn't feel like going down. I hadn't seen her in a decade. And the last time I had, I ended up in prison, and she built a life somewhere I wasn't. A lot of lies. A lot of hurt.

I flopped down on the futon, my breathing coming in deep gasps, calming in slow measure. Cory shouted something, but I had little time for him at that moment. I closed my eyes, trying to will the dregs of the dream away. Little by little, it faded, and my breathing calmed. The echo of breaking glass came to me, and I tensed, trying to ignore it. Instead, Cory's voice became strident, loud. I jumped from the bed and stopped.

Shards of glass on the floor glinted in the moonlight, shards of glass on the table shone wickedly. Someone had broken in through the fire escape and shattered Cory's jar. Whatever other purpose their little trip had, Regnos busting the place up probably bought them a distraction.

I stood for a moment, looking at the jar that had been my former lover's prison. Thought about the sound of rain on a roof, the smell of a park in summer. Thought about nights curled on the couch with Chinese and a bad movie. Tasted betrayal like bitter almond. I knew I should feel something more at the loss of someone I'd shared so much life with. Or maybe I'd taken on too much of the jailer, and caring was too much work. Or maybe I was just tired.

But now I had a loose soul, and a missing kitchen window. I grabbed a broom and swept the glass up, then taped an old pizza box over the window, making my shitty apartment somehow shittier. Isn't that always the way? No one ever breaks in to redecorate. Always chaotic evil, never chaotic good.

I went back to bed because growing boys need their sleep. And because my hands were throbbing from the cuts, and if someone wanted to break in a second time, I was honestly too damn tired to stop them.

I woke up to the sound of something ticking in my kitchen. My first thought was *bomb*. My second was the sun peeping in through the windows in a hazy pink half-light, telling me I'd got less sleep than I'd hoped. I rolled out of bed and stepped to the kitchen, stopping in my tracks. The cardboard had fallen from the window, and a crow strutted across the cheap linoleum of the table, its claws making the ticking sound. I sat heavily in the aluminum chair. *Witches*. I blew out an annoyed breath.

"Okay, Ivy sent you. What's she got to say?" I asked.

The bird glared at me with one beady black eye, cocked its head to the side. Crows are smart. They know how to use tools; they remember faces and hold grudges. There's a reason so many witches like them. They're avian mercenaries. It opened its beak.

"PAIN. BEWARE. MORE TO THINGS," it squawked.

"Is that it?"

"DIPSHIT."

I rolled my eyes and waved the bird away. Its message delivered, it took two long strides to the edge of the table and launched itself into the air, soaring from the kitchen, through the gaping window, and into the early dawn light. I cursed once under my breath and made some coffee.

3

You'd think I'd have better things to do than ruminate on the myriad of problems presented to me, especially under deadline, but not thinking in the past had got me into situations I'd rather not have had to deal with. So, I sat and thought. Someone didn't want me going after the girl. I didn't know if freeing Cory was a part of the plan, but the timing was more than coincidental.

While I thought, I ate a fried egg sandwich, washing it down with a pot of coffee, and when I'd finished, I showered, shaved, and dressed. It's less about the thing than the ritual.

I left the apartment and hopped a cab to the warehouse district. It was close enough to the water the scents of algae and fish permeated the air, accompanied by the tang of industrial solvents and food slowly spoiling. I'd arrived early enough the place was still mostly quiet.

It was the sort of place men with questionable morals made their personal amusement park. Everything from chop shops to sweatshops and anything between filled the corrugated steel buildings down there. For a minute, I had the mental image of the whole row going up in flames. I squashed the idea and hunkered down.

The warehouse sat squat and long at the end of a row of similar structures, the corrugated steel already drinking the light. Fans atop the roof spun, doing their best to cool the big storehouses, though the doors remained closed, and the high windows dark. The word KRUGER stood out in red and white across the side.

From where I sat, atop a frontage road running above the inset of the warehouse district, I saw a figure pacing the perimeter, though whether he was regular or private security, I had no idea.

I slid down the hill in stages, pausing every few feet to make sure I wasn't getting hung up on a piece of scrap, or making too much noise, timing my passage with the guard's around the back of the building. Once at the bottom, I waited in the shadow of another warehouse that smelled like someone had set off a herring bomb.

The guard rounded the corner, and I drew on Llyrial. I felt my blood rise, my cheeks flush, as I imagined the guard and I sweating in an alley. I only hoped he was distracted with the same thoughts.

I approached and smiled, and the guard smiled back. His jacket had 'Stephen' embroidered on the breast, and I moved in, watching his pupils dilate, his breathing come faster.

"Hi," I said.

I'm fantastic at flirting.

"Hi. What're you doing here?" he asked.

"I'm los—" I started, but Llyrial was in full mode now, and I could smell the lust on the man. The thing about a demon like this, it's not about orientation. It's about attraction. And Llyrial could draw the animal urge out of a block of wood, given enough time.

"There's an alley…" he began.

I followed him in, his hands already working the buckle of his uniform, pants bulging at the front. I released Llyrial, and called on Regnos, rage filling me. My fist lashed out before he could unzip, and the guard went down like a sack of bowling balls. I jogged to the head of the alley, looking both ways before stepping to the side door. I listened.

"And I say to you, lo, do we not feel?"

A chorus of voices raised in response. If this was a church service, I was about to interrupt communion in the rudest possible way.

"Lo, do we not bleed?"

More cheers. Whatever was going on was not what I'd expected.

"Lo, do we not ACHE?"

The voices reached a crescendo, and through it all, a deep keening wail. That had to be the girl. I stepped back and kicked the door by the latch plate. It shuddered, and then snapped open, smashing into the wall with an echoing crash. Five men turned to look at me, their leader, Cotton, standing on a scaffold. He held a knife in one hand, and in the other, a hammer. I smelled fear and misery and called on Regnos.

"HOLD HIM!" Cotton shouted, and the men charged as the little girl wept.

I put two down with hard strikes to the forehead, and though I knew my knuckles were going to ache in the morning, grinned. Rarely do I take pleasure in the demon's violence, but anyone who makes a child cry deserves a good smashing.

One of the goons—big, and smelly—caught me in the kidneys with a pipe. I went down, my head bouncing off the concrete with a smack. Stars danced in my vision, and Regnos snarled, pulling me up again. Blood oozed into my right eye as another came from the opposite direction, but the demon was in full swing, and caught his fist, snapping the bone in his forearm with little effort. He gave a scream and collapsed, coddling his arm.

Three down, and I didn't know where the little guy had gone, but big man was back in my face, hammering my torso with his pipe. I screamed as he cracked a rib or three, then I grabbed the pipe, reversing it and slamming it into his windpipe. It crunched with a sound like a plastic bag, and he wheezed out his last on the cold floor.

I took a second to get my breath, and number four hit me from behind again, a small knife slipping into my back. Luck was with me though—it was too short for spine or organ, and instead, I just bled all over their floor when I ripped it out.

With one final bestial growl, I rammed the knife into an eye gone wide with terror, the body toppling. Heedless of my own pain, I charged up the stairs in time to see the cultist raising his hammer over the little girl, her face a mask of terror.

I sped forward, watching the hammer fall in slow motion. Too late. I dove in front of her. The world went dark.

———

I t starts with a slamming drawer, a fist hammering into a wall. A shout. He stomps through the house until he finds me, rage written plain on his red face. His eyes are wide, his fists clenched. My stomach knots, and I step back.

"Where is it?" he seethes.

"What?"

"The roll of film. I had it in the desk." He's barely contained, moving closer.

"I don't know! I promise!"

"Did you take it? I know you took it. Damn kid, can't keep his hands off shit."

I'm shaking, already sure where this is going. I back up another step, but he advances, hot breath in my face.

"Liar!" he screams. Spittle flecks my face.

He grabs me by the throat, and my breath seizes as he picks me up. I struggle, chest heaving, throat burning, and he slams me into the wall, my head ringing with the impact.

"WHERE IS IT?" he shouts.

I try to wheeze out words, but only tears come, leaking from the corners of my eyes like pain overflowing. I thrash, struggle again, and he shakes me, my feet dangling. It seems no one should be this strong, this angry. I'm his child. His son.

He slams me into the wall again, and I realize I am also disposable. Panic and rage shudder through me, and I kick out, connecting with his thighs. He grunts and pushes me hard into the wall, and I kick again, heel slamming into his balls. He lets go with a grunt, dropping me to the floor.

I curl up and rub my throat, crying as he thunders away, his rage temporarily sated. My tears and choking sobs come hot, burning...

––––––

I woke in an alley, the taint of Xiphos' presence still swirling in my mind. I tasted pennies and alcohol and wondered where I'd been. Whenever that one came to the surface, all bets were off. I had little to no control over the demon and wasn't entirely sure how I'd ended up with it. The old man might have been able to tell me, if he didn't currently have a mouth full of grave dirt.

The rain had begun again, a thin drizzle, and when I sat up, a bottle rolled to the side, the label declaring it whiskey. I licked my lips and came to the realization that was where the similarity ended. It had been whiskey the same way you can substitute kerosene for gas.

I looked around, a slash of red catching my eye. It decorated the bricks of the alley in a bright Pollockian splash, and below it, the remains of Cotton, his pants ragged, suit coat soaked in gore. Empty sockets stared from a ruined skull.

As I inspected the body through bleary eyes, a dull ache announced itself in my wrists and knuckles, echoed a moment later by a sharp pain in my ribs. I knelt by the corpse and lifted the shirt, the sight of black and yellow bruises flowering over tattoos making my stomach do a loop.

Somehow, despite my misery, Xiphos had sought out a threat, and dealt with it. I dropped his shirt and peeked out of the alley. Ivy's building rose across the street, the lights on in her penthouse. So, I'd had enough sense to head somewhere familiar, at least, even if it wasn't home.

I turned back to the body, inspecting the tattoos again. Everyone had their own, though no two demons shared the same name. I counted rage, lust, hatred, and one more I didn't recognize. It bore a passing resemblance to madness, but the Enochian written in the circle twisted and barbed against itself, the lettering corrupted. I shuddered. Demons were one thing—bound and leashed, they made powerful allies. Demons had been angels, after all. But this—the letters squirmed and writhed, and as I watched, the center of the circle rippled, the flesh parting like a curtain.

A mouth pushed itself to the center of the red folds, a thick lolling tongue licking at the edges of the wound. It spoke, the words guttural nonsense.

I reeled back from the mouth as laughter pealed from the lips, the tongue dissolving as the collagen holding it together dripped in fat globs to the pavement. The teeth followed, falling to the asphalt, and making clinking sounds as the lips separated and plopped to the earth, squirming like plump worms before dissipating into the muck.

A car passed, tires shushing against the wet pavement, lights flaring as it passed, and I pressed myself against the wall, heart hammering. I had no urge to spend another moment in that close space with the body, but I'd have an even worse night if caught there with it. As soon as the car passed, I darted from the shelter of the alley and across the street, mashing the buzzer for Ivy's apartment.

Her voice came to me, wary. "Yeah?"

"IvyIvyIvyIvy..." I said, panic bleeding through.

"Man. Hold on."

The buzzer went off, and I yanked the door open, making sure to pull it shut behind me. As soon as I was sure it had latched, I took a moment to catch my breath and peer out of the glass.

Nothing followed from the alley, just an inky black between buildings. I tore my gaze away and made my way to the elevator, riding in silence until the doors opened on Ivy's apartment. It usually took a good deal to shake me, but this was wrong... invasive somehow. We invited our demons in, formed a bond with them. This was something else. A taint, corruption using the vessel.

Ivy opened the door, standing on the other side with a nine-inch knife and a scowl. I hesitated. I didn't feel like breaking the threshold and being turned into giblets. She looked me over, finally nodding.

"Come on in. Don't track mud onto my carpet," she said.

I hopped over the runner and onto the laminate of her kitchen. Water still dripped from me. She disappeared into the back and returned a minute later with a towel.

"Get dry. Then go shower. Got some clothes that'll fit you in the hall closet. You smell like a wet dog," she said.

She sat in the living room while I dried myself. I smelled lavender and heard her muttering something but stayed where I was. Once reasonably dry, I hit the shower. It was hot, and I let the warmth soak into my bruises and sore muscle. I did my best to scour the blood from under my nails, and only flinched when I closed my eyes, that alien mouth flashing in the darkness.

I climbed out and pulled a shirt, suit jacket and jeans from her closet. The clothing fit well. I transferred the contents of my pockets to the new clothes, then joined Ivy in the living room. She looked up from a bowl of something dark and thick on her coffee table, thin smoke rising from it. I plopped into the chair across from her, and she raised an eyebrow.

"Well, you smell better," she said.

"You don't seem surprised to see me."

"Saw what you did in the alley."

I grunted. I was doing my best not to think of the human ruin down there.

"Verbose tonight," she said.

"It's been a long couple of days."

She nodded and peered back down at the bowl.

"Any idea what that was?" I asked.

"Something. Something else."

"Not a great time to be cryptic."

She shrugged. "Can't get a bead on it. What'd Locke tell you?"

I fished the dollar from my pocket and dropped it on the table. She picked it up, a slight frown on her face.

"You look like you're trying to figure out a smell," I said.

"That was you," she said absently.

"What's up with the dollar?"

"It's a message, I think,"

"Which is?"

She shrugged and tossed it down, then rubbed her eyes. "No idea."

A rustle from the hallway had me on alert, and I tensed, my body sending up an aching flare. My shoulder knotted, and I gritted my teeth. A small shape emerged, dressed in an oversize white robe. I let myself relax into the chair again.

"The girl?" I asked.

Ivy nodded, and the little one ducked under her arm, looking at me with big brown eyes.

"She wasn't…"

"Dead? Near enough."

"Is she going to be all right?"

Ivy looked at the girl. "Back to bed, honey," she said.

The kid rubbed an eye and ignored her.

"Eventually," she said, answering my question.

"Why didn't you tell me?" I asked.

"I had to be sure you were you."

"What?"

"They marked you."

I stood and went to the mirror, pulling up my shirt.

"Turn around."

I did, craning my neck. That same corrupted Enochian I'd seen in the alley crawled in broken lines across my back. The cuts were pink and raw from the shower. I tried to read it, gave up.

"Shit," I said.

"King of understatement."

I pulled my shirt down and dropped onto the couch. The girl had cozied up to Ivy instead of going to bed.

"You okay, honey?" I asked. She nodded.

"Take her home, Ivy," I said, stretching out on the couch. I flipped Jacobs' card onto the table.

"What about you?" she asked.

"Sleepy."

"Boy, that is a three-thousand dollar couch," she warned.

"Fuck yo' couch," I muttered, half-asleep.

She laughed and led the girl out. Sleep hit me like a small train.

I woke in the dead of night, sweating into Ivy's cushions. Normally, you'd think that sort of thing would bother me, wrecking my friend's shit, but images still crept around my skull, killers in cloth woven from shadow, the warp and weft of nightmare. Most things I remembered. My father's rage. Near-death experiences.

But prison lurked in the shadows, and I only got glimpses of memory, random bursts from an erratic radio station. It was as if looking at it all, facing the entire thing head-on, would scar something in me deeper than all the other experiences of my life.

They still lingered, vivid splashes of color on a gray backdrop. A pool of blood, oozing under the crack of a 3-inch steel door. A shadow, swinging in the afternoon sunlight. Screams from the shower, more blood washing into the drain. The sound of a lock smashing into a skull. All these things, piling up, gaining weight. I shook my head and forced myself to get up, wandering to the window.

The street lay in blue shadow and half-light from the moon, streetlamps punctuating the dark like shouts in an empty room. Nothing moved. Not even the creepy fucker standing in the alley where I'd left the body. I did my best to appear as if I didn't exist. A minute dragged by, then two. He blinked, and then shuffled away, and I let out a breath, fogging the glass. I turned away and sat heavily on the couch, running my hands across my face and through my hair.

I needed a plan.

I pulled the dollar across the table, smoothing it out. A red spot marked Washington's cheek, and I rubbed at it absently. It didn't come out. A thought hit me, and I pulled away from the dollar. Vincent's dollar. Vincent's *cursed* dollar. I swore loud enough to wake the neighbors, and the door opened, Ivy strolling in. A frown creased her forehead.

"What's up, buttercup?" she asked.

"Motherfucker set me up."

"Who?"

"Vincent."

I gestured at the dollar, and she raised an eyebrow.

"It's cursed," I said.

She walked over to the coffee table and leaned in, then reached into her coat, and pulled out a stick of something that she fired with a lighter. Fragrance filled the air, and she moved it over the dollar. The smoke took on a deep purple, and the stick in her hand flared, then went out. Ivy made a low whistle.

"Wow. That guy's a dick," she said.

"How so?"

Granted, I knew Vincent was a dick already. Not specifically how.

"Someone dropped a blooding curse on it. You own it; you get your ass kicked until you give it up. Who gave it to you, anyway?" she asked.

"Your buddy—Locke?"

She shook her head. "I don't know what he'd have to do with thi—wait. Did you say Vincent?"

"Yeah."

"Vincent Cagliostro?"

"Yeah, everybody knows the guy. In the family way, a little vicious, pays well. Why?"

She shook her head. "You dumb motherfucker."

"What?"

She held up a hand. "Wait. Do you really not do research on your clients?"

"I'm discreet," I said defensively.

"Or dumb."

I opened my mouth to reply, and she held her hand up a second time.

"Wait wait wait. I want to savor this. You're so dumb you'd put a TV dinner in the VCR," she said.

"Hey—"

"You're so dumb it takes you an hour to cook instant rice."

"Wha—"

"You're so dumb if you saw a 'Wet Floor' sign, you'd stop and piss on it."

"Are you done?"

She was giggling hard enough to need to catch her breath, and I just watched her.

"Okay, Carrot Top. What's the deal?" I asked.

"The Cagliostros are notorious witch hunters, you stupid shit. Which you'd know if you ever bothered to read a book, or ask me a question that wasn't 'Gee Ivy, how do I walk and chew gum at the same time?'"

"Ahh, shit."

Ivy nodded, and walked to the fridge, rustling around. "So, you brought a witch hunter down on yourself," she said. "What's your plan?"

I shrugged. "I could just punch him 'til he falls down."

She came up out of the fridge with a carton of eggs, some cheese, ham, and mushrooms, and tossed a pan on the stove, mixing the ingredients with a brutal efficiency. I watched as she poured the mixture into the pan and tossed in some peppers from a jar.

"You're making us breakfast?" I asked.

"Yeah, you got somewhere to be?"

I shook my head and sat on the couch, staring at the dollar. I obviously couldn't go after Vincent directly, and I still had to learn where this new demon circle came in. I put my head in my hands, racking my brains. Ivy plopped a plate of steaming eggs and toast in front of me, alongside a glass of orange juice.

"Eat," she said.

I stuffed forkfuls of the food into my mouth, the eggs light and fluffy and gooey, the ham sweet and salty, the peppers spicy. It was all incredibly good. Ivy followed suit, and we ate in silence for a few minutes.

"What if you start at the bottom?" she asked.

"Like?"

"Like Jacobs. Seems like this whole thing started with him."

"How so?" I asked, not seeing the connection.

"He hired you, right?"

I nodded. "Yeah, but he seemed genuinely broken up about his girl," I said. "I'm not sure he's in on this. I think he might have been a pawn as well."

Ivy shrugged. "Find out what Vincent's got on him. Maybe you can turn it around. If it's not him, move up the chain. Locke'd be your next best bet."

"No solidarity among witches?"

She made a face. "Warlock. And not for the ones that sell out the people I like."

"Oh, you like me now?"

"I—look—you know what I meant."

"You like me, you want to kiss me, you want my booty," I sing-songed at her.

Ivy snorted and threw a piece of ham at me.

4

You can't always control when or with who you spend your time, but the times you can, I suggest you enjoy the small moments. We fell asleep on her couch, empty plates on the table before us, Ivy's feet across my lap, my head leaning into the plush cushions.

Sleep, for one of the rare moments in my life, remained blissfully devoid of nightmares. Maybe it was exhaustion. Maybe it was Ivy's news of Jacobs and his daughter's reunion, the girl no worse for wear. Maybe it was just that even demons need rest. Whatever the cause, when I woke to the gray filter of dawn and Ivy snoring, I was grateful.

I slipped out from under her and used the bathroom, then padded to the big glass windows. I paused, breath caught. The man from the night before stood across the street. He saw me and raised a tentative hand, and I stepped back, calling on Regnos, the demon awakening with a snarl. I rushed from the apartment, the door banging into the frame, and down the stairs, bursting onto the sidewalk. I charged across the asphalt and into the alley. Empty. No stranger, no body.

"What is it?" a voice asked from behind me.

I squealed a very manly squeal and pressed myself against the wall. Regnos made me strong. Stupidity made me brave. Sneaking up on me tended to negate both positive traits.

"Jesus, Ivy!"

"What?" she asked, the vision of innocence.

I opened my mouth, expecting something witty, something sarcastic. Instead, I squeaked.

"What?" Ivy asked again, concern replacing the smile playing across her lips.

"I don't—"

Pain blared into my body, an intruder on spiked feet, playing bagpipes. I groaned and went to my knees, wrapping my arms around my ribs.

"Jack!" Ivy shouted, but it was too late.

The pain swept in waves across nerve endings firing like sparks attempting to start a larger fire. I managed to open my eyes, meaning to wave Ivy away. Instead, I saw the lines etched into the concrete. Sweeping curves, Enochian keys, circles in circles, connected by more looping swirls. I recognized an awakening circle for what it was and only had time to collapse within the confines of the trap before memory and the demon's presence slammed into me.

———

"*Again!*" *Ramirez's slap rang in the cold stone room and I winced, a hand to my now-hot cheek.*

"*I don't understand what this is supposed to accomplish,*" *I said, trying not to make it sound like a whine.*

"*It's supposed to teach you control.*"

I sucked in a breath and looked around the room. Plain wood, stone floor, isolated. Escher's Rest was as far from civilization as a man could get without being off the grid entirely. He said it was safer that way, safer for the people in the city, safer for myself. So far, he'd been right.

So far, he had been right about a lot of things. My self-destructiveness, my selfishness, my self-loathing.

It was Ramirez who showed me the patterns, the tattoos that could bind my demons, make them something I owned, and not the other way around. It was Ramirez who held me in the awakening circles as we bound each—keeping my body healthy while the demon raged against its bonds. And now it was Ramirez kicking my ass while he tried to teach me to be more than the monster I'd been.

He hit me with a doubled fist, and I spat blood. Rage boiled within me, making my hands shake.

"Again?" he taunted.

"You hit like my grandmother."

"Your grandmother was a Golden Gloves champion?"

"Sailor. You smell like one, too."

He grinned. "Pendejo," he said, and punched me again.

It sent me reeling, and I staggered to one side.

"Is this how you'll do it?" he asked. "A smart mouth and a glass jaw ain't gonna help anyone out there. Or maybe you'll just bore them to death. Maybe you can run away, like a hurt bird, lead the bad men away? You'll make a good decoy. Maybe that's all you're good for. Ain't real smart. Ain't real—" he tried to finish. I didn't let him.

Regnos flared in my chest and I caught the old man with an uppercut. He lost contact with the earth for a moment, crashing down. I stood over him, knuckles aching, chest heaving. When he opened his eyes again, he laughed.

"Nice job, mijo," he said as he worked his way to his feet, a pained grimace flitting across his features.

His jaw was already starting to bruise. He clapped me on the back, and I spat another wad of bloody phlegm onto the stone and wondered why all the men I knew only knew how to teach through pain.

———

I snapped back to reality, Ivy crouched beside me, stroking wet hair away from my face.

"Jack," she said.

"Ivy."

"You okay?"

I didn't particularly know. Something in me moved, and I reached out to it, grabbed it by its metaphysical throat and pulled it into the light. It was yellow, the color of sandstone in the desert, with beady black eyes and thorny skin. I named it. Ramirez always said the naming was the most important part. It gave you power over a thing.

Praedolor.

It shivered and squirmed, and dissipated into its own pattern. I opened my eyes and sat up, and Ivy dropped back onto her haunches.

"What happened?" she asked.

"New roommate."

A smell came to me, thick and acidic, sharp. I moved my hand and noticed it was wet.

"I threw up?" I asked Ivy, my voice distraught.

She nodded. "Like Vesuvius."

"Ugh."

"Tell me about it. These are Manolos," she said, holding one vomit-spattered shoe out for inspection.

"Those were nice," I said.

"About four hundred dollars nice."

I stood, wiping myself off the best I could. "Ivy, if I had four hundred dollars, do you think I'd be sitting in a pool of my own puke?"

She shrugged. "Money can't buy class."

"Touché."

"Where to now?" she asked, standing as well, and shaking the vomit from her heels.

"Home, shower, and Jacobs."

"Good luck."

"Thanks. And hey, thanks for sitting with me."

She shrugged. "I had to roll you so you didn't choke. So, you owe me for that, too."

"Check's in the mail," I said, and started toward home.

5

I stood in the shower, trying to figure out what had happened in the alley. First, someone had cut Enochian into me. Next, the awakening circle, set by, I assume, the stranger who lured me out. Who was that? How was he connected? What the hell shampoo was I using? It smelled like strawberries. I stepped out and dressed in record time, then fished out Jacobs' card and gave him a call.

"'Lo?" he answered, voice a bit slurred.

"Mr. Jacobs?"

He cleared his throat. "Yeah, yeah. Sorry. Can I help you?"

"It's Jack Nyx. I was wondering if we could talk."

He cleared his throat again. "Yeah. After what you did for my girl, yeah. Same place?"

"That works," I said, and hung up.

The man was starting to grow on me. Anyone who can keep a phone conversation to under thirty seconds has a good chance of making it into my circle of friends. I left the apartment, taking the long way to Flamberge. I wanted Jacobs to sweat it out, to wonder what I was after. I may have liked the man, but like doesn't translate to trust.

It was a beautiful day. The closer I drew to the square with Flamberge, the louder the sounds of life grew, until they burst upon me as I exited a side street. I made my way to one of the tall tables, ordering a beer and a plate of street tacos, my stomach rumbling in agreement.

While I waited, I watched the crowd. Couples canoodled in the sunshine, and Llyrial let out a mournful sigh. I smiled and took a swig of beer, tipping the bottle up. A voice across the table made me put it down.

"Mr. Nyx?" the man asked.

Uh-oh. I knew that voice. Rather, I knew the *sort* of voice. Authority. It expected jumping whether you were a frog or not. I swallowed my beer and looked at the man across from me. Fit, forties, short hair, skin a deep black. He had the look of a small building someone had squeezed into a suit. A nose broken several times jutted from his face under deep brown eyes.

Part of me, the inmate from years ago, curled in on himself. Tried to pretend he didn't exist. If I liked Jacobs for his amiability, I disliked this man for what he represented. I tried to keep it from my face as I took the hand he offered.

"Detective Roberts, Mr. Nyx," he said by way of introduction.

I reached out and took his hand, his grip firm and sure.

"You have a minute?" he asked.

The waiter set the plate of tacos next to me and disappeared. I gave the food a longing look.

"Go ahead and eat. This won't take long," Roberts said.

I picked up a taco and bit into it, beef and lime and cheese and cilantro making happy food sex in my mouth.

"You know a Mark Jacobs, Mr. Nyx?" he asked.

I nodded; my mouth full of joy.

"Where were you an hour ago?" he asked.

I set the taco down, finished my bite. "In my apartment, making a call to Mr. Jacobs. Why?"

"He's dead, sir. Can you account for your whereabouts the past hour?"

"I took a walk around the city. I'm sure someone saw me."

He gave me a look that said he was weighing what I'd said. Then, he picked up my beer, took a swig, and nodded. He relaxed visibly. I did not. I was going to need a new beer. Who does that?

"Look. I know it wasn't you. If it were you, you'd be covered head to toe in about a gallon of gore. But I need you tell me what your relationship to Mr. Jacobs was."

Great. So, one literal dead end. My brain screamed this was Vincent's work. My gut sank with another realization, and my mouth took over.

"Is the girl okay?" I asked.

"She's fine. Was out for the day with a relative."

"What'll happen to her?"

He shrugged, noncommittal. "DHS, maybe. Maybe her aunt takes her. You really care that much?"

Relief flooded me. "I'm still human. What kind of animal doesn't care about the kid?"

He looked at me for a long moment, seemed to weigh something. Finally, he nodded and continued. "How'd you know Mr. Jacobs?"

"I did an odd job for him."

"What kind?"

I sighed. Sandbagging wasn't going to help anyone. "Someone took his daughter. I got her back."

"How?" The detective took another sip of my beer. My tacos were getting cold.

"Mostly punching, to be honest," I said.

"Who took her?"

I shrugged, tried to pretend I didn't know. "Bunch of crazies out on the docks. I'm sure they're gone now."

Roberts finished my beer, setting the bottle down. He pulled a card from inside his jacket pocket and pushed it across the table to me. "Call me if you hear anything. And don't up and leave town."

"Am I a suspect then?"

"I'm just saying, skipping town after I asked you questions about a dead man is bad form."

"I *am* a model citizen."

Roberts snorted and disappeared into the crowd. I didn't doubt he knew about my record. Whether he cared remained to be seen, but I'd be stupid to think it didn't matter. I tucked his card away, then ordered another beer and finished the tacos. You can call it cold, but I neither knew the man nor owed him a thing. I'd spent most of my life walking around with a combination of guilt and debt riding my spine like a coked-up monkey. I'd put the one to bed and paid the others. I was going to enjoy my damn lunch.

———

I sat back, watching the crowd but not seeing them. I didn't know who wanted Jacobs dead, but I thought I might know why. My gut said he would've had some answers someone wasn't prepared for me to have. That left me two choices, neither of which I was excited about.

I could go and talk to Locke again, or I could go back to the cult headquarters and look for clues. Both had their hazards. Locke had options at his fingertips if I pissed him off. He could pull my soul out like a piece of taffy or burn me down where I stood. He was also the one who gave me the dollar, so I didn't feel like we stood on solid ground. Which left option two—back to the warehouse. If I took my time getting there, assuming the cops were their usual thorough selves, it would be empty.

I paid the check and left the waiter a hefty tip. I didn't know if having a cop show up at one of your patron's tables was bad for business, but I couldn't imagine it was a boon. The market faded behind me as I made my way to the busier streets, hoping to hail a cab. I stepped from a side street onto the main drag, cars and people jostling for attention and position. I raised a hand, whistling loud, and for once, a car stopped right away. Skeletons and dice decorated the interior, and I smiled.

"Where to?" the cabbie asked.

"Docks. Take your time."

He put the cab in gear, and we lurched into traffic. It was a long ride, and I was still tired. I fell into a light nap as we made our way across town.

———

"*W*here are you going?" I ask.

She turns her head just enough to answer, purse on her shoulder, hand on the door. My stomach churns with anxiety.

"To your grandmother's. I'll be back in a bit," she says.

"Can I come?" I ask, the question out before I can stop it, trying to hold onto my fear, trying not to let it shake my voice like a tree in a summer storm.

She shakes her head. "Stay here. I'll be back in a bit."

The door closes, and I'm left alone with the silence building in the home, punctuated only by heavy tread, by the excitement of announcers on the TV hushed by the distance of rooms. I move on tenterhooks, sliding between rooms, feet arched on tiptoe, willing myself to be a shadow, willing myself to breathe as quietly as possible as the curses start, to not breathe, to sink into the wood and cease to be, if only for a time.

His voice comes to me, sharp with anger, the edge a warning.

"Get me a beer," he says.

I turn around, toward the fridge, toward the fuel for his fire, and pull the bottle from the interior, the glass cold against my palm. I stare out the window, at the place where my mother's car would sit, at the emptiness embodied there and within me, and clench my eyes tight.

"Today!" he yells from the other room. I jump, and on legs weary with fear, start back.

———

I woke from my doze in time for the cab to grind to a halt. I got out, tossed more money than I could afford to the cabbie, and made my way down the hill. The warehouse was as abandoned as I'd hoped. I mean, the rats were still there, but everything else remained the same. There were signs of recent disturbance—fresh tracks in the dirt, the door left ajar, but I chalked that up to typical police work, and let myself in.

The space was much the same as before—wide floor, steel-wrought scaffolding. I climbed the stairs to the platform where I'd confronted the priest and looked around. The altar had been disassembled, the bloodstains scrubbed, though several suspicious brown blotches marred the rusty steel. I knelt, looking under a small overhang on the walkway, hoping for a clue or any sign of how all this connected.

A scrap of paper caught my eye, and I snatched it, unfolding and smoothing out the creases. A circle decorated the wrinkled white—clean lines, nearly obsessive order, even in the Enochian. This was true angelic script. What the hell was something like that doing here?

I sighed and sat back on my haunches, unsure of what this meant. Sure, someone was pulling the cult's strings, but this got me no closer. I moved to stand, and something cold and hard pressed against my skull behind the ear.

I froze.

There are few things a man remembers permanently in life. First kiss, first fuck, first fight. First time someone presses a Glock 19 against your head. I sat very still and raised my arms. My heart hammered in my ears and I took slow breaths to control the panic threatening to shake my hands from my wrists.

"You stupid motherfucker. He said you'd come back, but I didn't believe it."

"Locke?" I said, the word an exhalation of exasperation.

"Sorry, Locke's not home. But if you check the dumpster behind the 7-11, you can probably reach him," he said. "Now get up."

I felt a piece click into place. Someone got the drop on the warlock, killed him, then this goon took his place. I felt better I wouldn't have to try to fist fight a wizard. Not great, considering the corpse and the barrel against my skull, but better. I stood; hands still laced behind my head. I tried to turn to look, but the barrel of the Glock dug a furrow into my scalp.

"Where we going?" I asked. "Is it Disneyland? I can't *wait* to see Mickey," I said.

"You'll find out. You pissed in the big boy's Cheerios when you rescued that girl. But that's your problem. We can correct your fuckups, but you can't correct being shit-for-brains."

I felt the pistol leave my skull for a moment and knew what came next. I don't know if you've ever been pistol-whipped, but it's not pleasant, and it sure as shit isn't what they show in the movies. Best-case: bleeding and a mild concussion. Worst case: bleeding and brain damage. Pistols are heavy, and I didn't care to catch one with my already-lumpy noggin.

I called on Regnos and felt rage flood up from below, adrenaline surging through my system, muscles tensing. I ducked and snapped back, my head hitting not-Locke in the ribs. Air blew out of him in a gust of curses, and I spun, grabbing the hand with the pistol.

Regnos snarled, and I snapped the man's wrist, white bone breaking from the skin like a bird bursting from its cage. Sure, it was more like someone smashing a sausage with a hammer but give me a break. I'm a cut-rate detective, not a poet.

I pulled him close to me while the pistol clattered to the ground and brought my knee into the inside of his thigh, connecting with tender skin and balls. He collapsed, cradling his injured parts, and I pushed Regnos back, fighting for control before I did something we'd both regret. I knelt next to him.

"Who are you?" I asked.

He coughed once and vomited, a thin yellow gruel. Maybe I ruptured something with that kick. I didn't care. I grabbed him by the hair and yanked his head back.

"Maandig!" he shouted. "Ramon, man."

Tears leaked from his eyes. I shook him a little.

"Did you kill Locke?" I asked.

"No, man, no. He was already dead. some guy just paid me to pass you the dollar, rough you up if I thought you were getting too close. You fucked up my hand, man."

"What about Jacobs?"

"Who?" he said. "My hand is real fucked up, man."

"Yeah. Guns are bad for your health. What'd the guy who hired you look like?"

"I dunno, man, it came through some lady."

"Blonde? Real proper?"

He nodded and retched again. I dropped his head and sat back on my heels.

"What're you gonna do, man? You gonna kill me?" Ramon asked.

"What? No," I said. "But I am gonna leave you here for a while. You gotta learn not to play with guns. Okay?" He didn't answer. "Night sweetie," I said.

I punched him in the forehead, and he went down with a groan.

I left the building and the bleeding man behind.

6

I made a beeline for Ivy's. I didn't know how to get in touch with the blonde woman, but I had Jacob's card, and she'd touched that, which meant she'd a left a piece of herself behind. Ivy claimed she didn't know how to find things, but I reasoned this was a person, not a thing, and they'd left soulstuff behind, Ivy's specialty.

I knocked on her door, and she opened it right away, a flat expression on her face.

"Hey," she said and tilted her head to her left.

"Hey. Can I come in?"

"Now's not great," she said.

"Why? Do you suddenly have a boyfriend? Girlfriend?"

She jerked her head again.

"Oh, right," I winked. "*Special* friend."

Ivy rolled her eyes and moved out of the way as Tall, Blonde, and Manicured stepped into view. She had a pistol in one hand and a carved rod of what looked like birch in the other. It came to a sharp point, and she wielded it like a spear.

"Mr. Nyx. Glad you could join us," she purred.

"You have got to be the stupidest bastard on the planet," Ivy said as I stepped in and the woman closed the door.

"What?"

She jerked her head to one side. "*This* is a signal."

"Oh."

The woman with the pistol waved us over to the couch and we sat down. She took the chair opposite us.

"Let's all have a nice chat, shall we?" she asked.

I eyed the rod in her hand, unconcerned with the gun. "What's with the stick, Brunhilda?"

She gave me a thin smile and gestured with the pistol at Ivy.

"Tell him," she said.

Ivy swallowed. "It's a Heartspike. If she lets it go, it will find the fastest way to its target and rip a hole in their chest to get at their heart."

"Oh good. My day wasn't horrific enough already," I said. "So, what do you want to chat about?"

"Mr. Cagliostro is not happy with the operation your friend here has set up in the middle of his city," she said. "As a result, he'd prefer if she packed up post-haste, and relocated somewhere else. You understand, this is a generous offer from a man of his stature."

"And if I don't?" Ivy asked.

"If you don't, well... Mr. Cagliostro has authorized me to move you," she said, and waggled the Heartspike.

The dollar still sat on the table, untouched. I looked at it, wondering just how much the blonde monster knew about Cagliostro. I didn't think he was the type to share everything. Why would he? A cursed item he could pass to his enemies at any time, an item guaranteed to bring them misfortune and bodily harm? I'd keep that shit close to the vest.

Well, not in a pocket.

I looked at Brunhilda. "Deal," I said.

Ivy's mouth dropped open and she shot me a look that could

have withered a strong man's heart. "Motherfucker, are you kidd—"

"Look, no one wants Ivy dead. You're not a killer, are you? That jacket says Armani, and you don't want blood all over that."

The blonde looked at me, a smirk on her face, one eyebrow raised. "Perhaps."

"Perhaps is good. We can work with perhaps. So, how about it? Ivy packs up, and you and Cagliostro go back to bumping evil uglies."

She snorted. "Fine. I will need a sign of your good faith however, Mr. Nyx. I don't trust just any demon-possessed lunatic that wanders in."

Ivy sat to the side, throwing daggers with her eyes. Her lips moved, and I sincerely hoped she wasn't tossing a curse my way. I pretended to cast about and find the dollar on the table.

"How about this?" I asked. "I'll even sweeten the deal."

I pulled a pin from a glass dish on the table and pricked my thumb, then smeared it across the dollar. I stood, hands out, and approached, holding it out to the woman. She lowered the pistol, a spark passing between us as she took the dollar. Her hand twitched, and the pistol fell from numb fingers. I took my shot and grabbed her wrist, snapping it upward. The bone shattered, and she screamed. I'd have to talk to Regnos about her obsession with breaking wrists. I grabbed the Heartspike, and the woman bolted, disappearing out the door. The spike slipped, my hands slick with sweat.

"Ivy!" I shouted in warning.

Unfortunately, the woman's last impulse must have been to change its target, and it slammed into my chest, pain blossoming outward from the point of impact like dye in water. I had enough time to feel my torso and stomach grow sticky, hear the crack of my sternum, and Ivy scream a word of power that blissfully knocked consciousness from my skull.

I don't know what death looks like. I don't know if it's a chorus of angels, a fiery pit, or a falling black curtain, and the only thing after is nothing. I did know I'd been in these cold gray corridors before. The Maze. Where demonites trained for control. Doors opened down the hall, and shadowed figures entered, lumbering and drifting.

I stood, bones creaking, and waited only a moment—long enough for the figures to resolve and my stomach to dive-bomb my feet like Buddy Holly heading for the mountainside. My father, his brow beetled, heavy sledge heads where his hands had been, what was once his tongue now an asp, its own tongue flickering as he opened his mouth and bellowed. Beside him, my mother, her head the wrong way, a caul of flesh covering her skull, thorns running the length of her black dress.

I ran.

The hall stretched to oblivion, or at least it seemed that way. As I went, I passed door after door, only stopping long enough to check one here, another there. They stood locked tight, and I fled as the deep bass rumble of my father's voice drew closer, chips of stone raining on my head as he beat the walls with his fists. Over my other shoulder, I heard screeching as my mother stretched her arms, a low wail escaping the caul encasing her skull, her nails ripping into the walls.

I poured on speed, breaking into a sprint and putting distance between myself and my tormentors, legs quivering, lungs burning. I ran as far as I could, and then turned, trying to call on my demons, but no answer came. In desperation, I tore at the nearest door. Some deity must have felt merciful, because the door flew open, and I ducked inside, letting it slam behind me.

Ivy stood there, in a circle of light, screaming. At who or what, I didn't know. Then she drew a fist back and punched me in the chest. Once. Hard. The action made my body spasm, and outside the door, the bellowing and wailing rose to a fever pitch, the sound of thorn and hammer ripping at the wood. Ivy hit me again, and the world flickered. I dropped to my knees.

"Ivy!" I shouted.

She reached down, her fist entering my chest and tugged. Searing pain flashed through me, the door shattering behind me. The world went black.

————

When I surfaced, Ivy stood over me, the Heartspike in one gory hand. Sweat clung to her face, and veins stood out in stark contrast to the whites of her eyes. I blinked up at her.

"Ivy?" I asked.

She sobbed once and threw away the spike, then collapsed on me, her frame shaking, tears mingling with the blood on my shirt. I went back to sleep. Or as close to sleep as the amount of blood I'd lost would allow. Sometimes you take a nap, sometimes you take a small coma.

7

I woke with a pounding headache and an ache in my chest. Something held my ribs tight, and I lifted the light sheet, finding Ivy'd stripped me to the waist and bound me with a long strip of gauze. Red seeped into the center, Regnos' tattoo peeking out the sides. I groaned. Until the wound healed and I could get the lines re-inked, my control would be tenuous. I'd have to watch how I handled things for a while unless I wanted a runaway demon in my head, or to trigger Xiphos.

Ivy appeared in the doorway of the guest room, a plate in her hand. She stopped when she saw I was awake, her face a mask.

"You're up," she said. "What's on your mind?"

"Xiphos," I said.

Her lips made a tight line. "Do you know what that word means?"

I shook my head, tried to rub sleep from my eyes.

"It's the Greek word for a god of death."

"Fantastic," I said.

"Feeling any better?" She asked, changing the subject.

"Yeah," I cleared my throat and sat up. "How long was I out?"

"About a day."

"Huh. Hungry."

She handed me the plate, a peanut butter and potato chip sandwich on it—one of my favorites—and a glass of milk. She watched me for a minute, and then spoke.

"You got lucky," she said.

I shrugged, my mouth full.

"I've always said you were dumb, but not suicidal. What the fuck were you thinking?" she asked.

I finished the sandwich and chugged the milk. "I was thinking I didn't want you to die."

My turn to change the subject. "What about the woman?" I asked.

"Gone."

"Thank the small gods." I let that hang in the air for a moment. "I think they're going after the girl. Or they've got her already."

Ivy didn't answer, and instead looked away. As she turned her face, I caught a glimpse of dark circles under her eyes, frizz in her hair. I swallowed my next sentence and put a hand on her shoulder. She didn't turn back, but did put her hand on mine. We sat for a moment, silence surrounding us like an old friend.

Finally, she squeezed my hand and sniffed, once, then turned.

"What next, wonder boy?"

I shrugged and swung my legs from the bed, testing my weight. My chest and ribs sent up lances of pain, but I stood anyway, Ivy reaching out for me in case I fell. I swayed, and she pressed one hand into my hip, steadying me. I smiled my thanks and evened out, taking a breath.

I ached, and tiredness swept through me like a slow fire, but I could move. Which meant I could do something about the situation. Ivy stood, her hand still pressing down gently on my hip. Warm. Right, like it was supposed to be there.

She opened her mouth, and I moved to cover it with mine. For a moment, she met the pressure of my lips with her own. She tasted of fruit. Then, she pulled back, a laugh on her lips, and like that, the tension broke.

"Jesus, Jack," she laughed.

"What?" I asked, my cheeks red.

"You've got a hole in your chest."

"Yeah, good point," I said, and looked at the floor.

"No, this is," she said, and thumped me in the wound. Pain flared through my chest and I dropped onto the bed holding my sternum.

"Ow!"

"Yeah, ow. Keep it in your pants, fuckbrain. Now come on, let's go see a man about some bullshit."

I pulled on a shirt and followed her out, wincing at the echo of pain still rippling through me.

8

We sat in Ivy's living room, drinking whiskey and thinking. I mean, I always think a little better while mildly altered. She leaned back, legs crossed at the ankles, head tilted toward the ceiling.

"What's your plan?" she asked.

"I had planned on busting into his bar and beating him until he looked like red paste."

"And now?"

"I can't risk overtaxing Regnos. Xiphos might come out. Or the new one," I said. "I have no idea what the consequences would be. And Llyrial is only any good if I want to fuck him to death."

"Which leads me to another question," she said. "Why haven't you ever turned your little lust ray on me? Not good enough?"

Her eyes flicked over me, head to toe. I couldn't tell if she was sizing me up or playing with me.

"It's not that," I protested. "You're a friend, Ivy. And to be honest, the little bastard creeps me right the fuck out. I don't even have any idea why I'm saddled with him."

It was the truth. Demonites get the demons they get. It takes some major mojo to get more. Which is what bothered me about the addition of Praedolor. I didn't know how a vanilla like Cagliostro managed to bind the thing to me. Which meant he couldn't be the last link in the chain. Someone either owed him something, or someone owned him. I just wondered who.

She took a sip of her drink and waved a hand. "Just fuckin' with you. I know you and Cory had it hard at the end."

I was silent for a minute, reliving old fights, old hurts in the span of heartbeats. Ivy broke the quiet.

"C'mon," she stood. "Let's go out, get you out of your head."

I followed her to the door, and down to the parking garage. She hit a button on a fob and a Mercedes beeped nearby.

"Stylin'," I said.

"Stylin'? Are you a Zach Morris fanboy?"

"Zach Morris is trash," I said, and got in the car.

———

I vy pulled the car up outside a huge home with a brick facade, white pillars, and a wide porch. I hadn't paid much attention as she drove. Instead, I just watched the city pass and let my thoughts drift, in an attempt to wall off the pain seeming to have set up shop in my bones. I blinked when we came to a stop, taking in our surroundings.

"Where are we?" I asked.

"Vincent's house."

"WHAT?" the word echoed in the car. "Are you insane?"

She shrugged. "He came to my house, so we're coming to his."

"I just told you it's not like I can kick in his door."

"Er..." she said. "I sort of kind of did a thing."

"What?"

"I stitched a talisman into your chest," she said in a rush. "It'll let you control Regnos' strength without going all wibbly-wobbly insaney-waney. I knew it was going to be an issue when I saw the damage to your tattoo."

"Holy shit, woman. Boundaries."

"Look who's talking, Biff Meatmissle."

We got out of the car. "I'm just saying, you did it first. You ever hear of informed consent? This has got to be some sort of HIPAA violation."

"You ever hear of shutting the fuck up?"

I didn't have a reply to that, so I snapped my jaw closed. We stood in front of the gate to Vincent's home. If the outside was any indication, he was doing better trade at The Stone than I'd imagined. I wondered how many pies he had fingers in.

"What kind of nasty shit you think he's got in here?" I asked.

She shrugged and pulled a small glass jar from her pocket. It was full of glitter.

"What're you gonna do, annoy him to death?" I asked.

She tossed it over the gate and onto the drive, where it shattered with a tinkling sound, glitter expanding in a cloud. As it did, small bursts of static shot between the flakes. The gate made a screeching sound and popped open. I looked at Ivy, one eyebrow raised. She grinned at me.

"Hexed, motherfucker," she said, and walked in.

———

The grounds to Vincent's home were empty. A Maserati in the drive, the hood cool, birds in the trees, and a squirrel zipping through a bush. No alarms buzzed; no guards leveled automatics at us. I took the direct route, climbing the porch and peering in the windows. The place appeared empty.

"Got a way to open the lock?" I asked.

Ivy shook her head.

"Guess we do it the old-fashioned way," I said.

I kicked the door, hard, breaking the lock away from the

jamb, and it slammed into the wall, smashing drywall. Rizzo stood from the chair he'd been occupying and lifted the shotgun he held.

"Good night," he said, and pulled the trigger.

The rock salt blasted into my skin, embedding itself with an aggression I hadn't before thought possible from a mineral. I screamed and dropped to my knees, blood running from a dozen holes. I was also pretty sure it'd aggravated the one in my chest. Literally rubbing salt in a wound is a shitty thing to do.

Ivy shouted something and a flash of light seared my retinas, dazzling me for a moment. I tried to get up, forcing my legs to work, but another blast knocked me to my back, and I squirmed on the ground in pain. I rolled to one side, trying to keep moving, to not let the pain settle in, but a boot caught me in the ribs, and I screamed again. I managed to blink away the light just in time to see another boot coming.

Ivy shouted a second time, something dark, with thick guttural syllables. The word hung in the air like greasy smoke, and the foot fell as the rest of the body exploded into a shower of meat and gore. I rolled onto my back; the pain drawing tears from my eyes. Ivy appeared over me.

"Shit. You okay?" she asked.

"I don't think so," I said as the skin on my back rippled like a wave.

"Is it—"

"Get out, Ivy."

"What?"

"GET. OUT," I screamed, as my back tremored again. "DEMON."

Her eyes widened, and she bolted as new waves of pain rolled me onto my stomach. I felt flesh tear, blood rolling and pooling into the small of my back. With a sound like a ripping sail, the demon tore its way free from the circle, bounding onto the tile floor with clicking claws. It leaned down and looked at me, head on one side, then bounded off, fading into the aether as it moved through shadow.

Praedolor was free, and I had no idea where it was headed. I'd likely spend more time worrying about the preternatural engine of death traipsing about the city, but right about then, I was preoccupied with a wave of agony. It shut my brain off like a meter man with a grudge, and the world blacked out.

9

When I woke again, it was to Roberts sitting beside me on a curb, smoking. A set of handcuffs pinned my hands behind my back and cut into my wrists. Agony strobed and roared through me like a crowd at a parade and I vomited. Roberts patted me on the back, sending more aches across my body.

"Sit up, sport. There you are."

I coughed once and looked at him. "How fucked am I?"

He drew on the cigarette and threw the butt away, blowing a plume of smoke into the breeze. "Depends. Did you break into a prominent crime lord's home and kill his lieutenant?"

I shook my head. "That was a friend. I just broke a ketchup bottle. That's why I'm all red. Might've cut myself a little."

Roberts chuckled, and then looked off into the distance. "So, here's the problem. I don't like Vincent. I don't think you're a terrible person. But. I do think I just found you in his home amid a shitload of blood and damage. So, I need to blame someone. I could blame Rizzo *if* Vincent weren't around to contradict my story."

"Are you commissioning a murder, detective?"

He shrugged. "I'm just saying, the way I see it, there are two positions open. At the cemetery or the prison. Only need one person to fill it though."

"And you're not picky?"

"I'm not picky."

I sighed. "All right. Get these cuffs off me."

He reached back and ratcheted them off, then patted me on the back again. I winced and stood. My vision did a little spin, and I grabbed a corner of a building to avoid eating an asphalt hors d'oeuvre.

"Go on, Mr. Nyx. Don't let me see you again," Roberts said.

I wanted to say something witty. Instead, I just limped around the corner and down the street.

10

Ivy's door was open when I got to her apartment. I heard voices within and stepped through, nerves tensed, ready to rip whoever I found inside to shreds. I'd been keeping Regnos at a low rage to take the edge off the pain, and my nerves were tuned tighter than piano strings.

I rounded the corner in a rush and stopped short. Ivy sat across from the man I'd seen a few days ago in the alley. His skin was pale, and thin scars ran across several parts of his exposed flesh. He smiled gently.

"Jack. You should sit down," she said.

"Why?"

"This is Cory."

I didn't say anything. What can you say when a ghost walks in? *Hey, how's it been? Uh, sorry I stuck you in a bottle like a cut-rate genie, but you did kill my pops.* Likely not. I sat in Ivy's chair while she and Cory sat on the couch. She brought me a tall glass of water and I sipped it while they talked.

"So, Vincent had Rizzo break Cory out, then they stuck him in this body and blackmailed him to trap you," Ivy was saying.

I finished the water and set the glass down.

"Still doesn't explain why he killed the old man," I said. "Or the body in the alley. Or why Rizzo didn't kill me in my sleep instead of all this."

"You were never the target. Vincent's got plans. Everyone else is a tool. The body was one of those," Cory said. "As far as Ramirez, the old man was using you."

"Who told you that?" I asked.

"Vincent."

"Vincent," I spat. "Figures. What kind of plans?"

Cory shrugged. "Says he got himself a backer now. Big one. Isn't afraid to make a move."

"Smells like bullshit," I said. "I don't know why you let him in here, Ivy."

Pain warred with sadness on Cory's face. It wasn't the one I was used to, but I knew the emotion all the same.

"What else do you know?" I asked.

He shrugged. "They let me go once I helped wake the demon."

"Okay," I stood. "Congratulations on being alive, but I've got a cop breathing down my neck."

"What?" Ivy asked.

I told her what happened after she'd escaped.

"You can't take on Vincent," Cory said.

"Why not? It's that or end up in prison again. Or dead."

Cory looked at Ivy. "Reason with him," he said.

She raised an eyebrow. "Man's got a job to do."

"Thank you, Ivy," I said. I stood and stretched.

"Please, make sure he doesn't try to kill you or get himself killed," I said.

Ivy nodded. Cory opened his mouth and shut it. I left.

I had time to think on the way to the bar. Too many things didn't add up. Cory's lies felt like lies he'd told before. Like a kid rehearsing lines for a school play. And if I hadn't believed him after Ramirez's death, I don't know what would move me to now. A new body doesn't mean a clean slate if the soul inside is still dirty. It bothered me that I knew he held something back but couldn't sus it out.

Regardless, I had enough ghosts and demons of my own without needing live ones. I had a girl to find, and a man to beat senseless.

11

I formulated a plan on the way to The Stone. Which I put into action by waiting until the bar locked its doors and then kicking said doors in. Vincent had cleared out the tables, leaving an open space in the middle of the floor. *How convenient,* I thought.

"Vincent Cagliostro!" I shouted.

A sound came from the back, and I turned toward the office door in time to see it blow off the hinges. Something massive barreled through, slamming into me, spikes on its flesh ripping into my skin and reigniting pain from still-fresh wounds. I hit the ground in a heap, and the thing skidded to a stop, heavy breathing filling the air. I rolled to my stomach, seeing Vincent transformed.

He stood seven feet, razor-sharp bone radiating from his body like the quills of a porcupine. His skin had turned a sickly off-white. He smiled, and a tongue roughly the size of a chihuahua lolled from his mouth. I'd guessed this is what had happened to Praedolor, but the demon had become too strong for Vincent, resculpting his flesh, ruling his mind.

The demon attacked again, black claws tearing a chunk from

my side. Blood spill down my side, filled my waistband, and I lashed out, Regnos snarling at the fore. I connected, barely, and still I felt bone break on the demon. Praedolor bellowed and spun in place, talons clipping my face. Blood flooded my vision, and I sincerely hoped he hadn't got the eye as well. I tried again for the beast, but it had already moved.

I spun in place, unable to see fully, wiping my eye. Exhaustion threatened to weigh me down, but the rage demon was in full swing. Anger is a better stimulant than even amphetamine. An impact flung me into the wall, and I screamed for the third time that day as something inside tore. I struggled to my feet, swaying, then leaning into the wall for support.

"Praedol—" I started.

My vision swam and

Summer days spent fishing. Building rockets and watching them fly into the blue above, the puff of smoke ejecting the parachute like a signal of trouble. Sitting side by side, trying to puzzle out games and riddles.

I shook my head to clear it, to hold it at bay.

"Praedolor," I said.

The demon, a pale blur in the corner of my eye, skidded to a halt. It turned its head toward me on creaking tendons. I grimaced and straightened, wiping blood from my face. I'd named it. I could handle it. As my mother was fond of saying, *I brought you into this world, I won't hesitate to take you out.*

"Praedol—" I started for the third time.

The demon screamed, a sound making my head ache like I'd just come off a three-day bender, and part of me wished for the whiskey to back it up. I stared the thing that had been Vincent in the eye once again and set my jaw, straightened my back.

And despite these things, despite these attempts at normalcy, the struggle with toxicity sending out flares motivating limbs and mouths in spasms of violence, the words that fly when fists don't, the hammer blows to self-esteem and ego, the knuckles bruising skull and tender flesh still come. I see it again, and in the context of those attempted moments of reconciliation, it makes the pain all that much worse, bitterness following the sweet, a chocolate so dark as to burn the tongue.

And still the demon stood.

"PRAEDOLOR," I shouted, something in my throat snapping.

I tasted copper. The demon started, body jerking as if hit with a live wire, and I met pale lidless eyes, red threads of vein running through the sclera. I stared it down as I approached, the world wavering. I felt our minds connect as my mouth formed the words to bind it, and I fed it everything.

Every pain. Every sorrow. The blasted landscape of my life laid bare like a nerve flayed fresh from muscle and sheath. The demon flinched, and I bore down, showing it every single rotten stinking moment, every shining bauble of triumph, and it cowered as black rage and pain poured from me like a busted sewer pipe. The world flickered, and darkness rose up to swallow me.

He raises a hand, curled into an instrument of pain, and rage tears through me. No more. I lash out, small fists connecting with his throat, small feet connecting with his groin. He staggers back, and I scream as I attack him, a deep wellspring of rage and sadness no longer held back by the antiquated dam of respect. Sharp teeth spill his blood, raw throat screams its sorrow. Some things you don't get back. Some things, once bled, stain stone indefinitely.

The rage built to a crescendo, and I felt something black and vicious rise in me. I went away for a time.

———

When I woke, it was on the floor. Ivy had torn up my shirt to stop the bleeding and knelt over me. Vincent huddled in the corner, weeping, alone. He made half-intelligible animal sounds through the tears, and his hands pawed pointlessly at the wooden floorboards.

"Where'd you come from?" I managed to rasp out when she let me sip from a water bottle.

"Cory gave me the slip, so I decided to follow you."

"Vincent?"

"Broken."

"The girl?"

Ivy shook her head. I cursed.

"Any trace of her?" I asked.

"I ran a locator but couldn't get a lock. I'm not the best with that anyway, but it should've screamed if she was here. I got nothing."

I laid my head down. I hurt all over. So, Cory had lied, and the girl was in the wind. But at least no one was trying to eat my face. Ivy leaned into my view of the ceiling.

"Not bad work, for a white boy, I guess," she said.

"Not bad w—?"

"Shush, honey. Take the compliment."

For once, I shushed. Maybe it was the blood loss, but she looked lovely in the half-light.

12

I woke in my own bed, Ivy puttering around the kitchen. It sounded like someone had let an angry drummer into my cabinets. I groaned. Pain washed over me like an old friend returning from a long trip. If that friend liked lingering hugs and was covered in thorns. Ivy banged another pan, and I winced. She stomped into the room brandishing a saucepan.

"What is this?"

I rubbed my forehead and squinted. "A pan?"

She shot me a glare. I bit off another retort. Probably not a good idea to mess with someone with the strength to carry me to bed. I blinked, then looked under the sheets. And had apparently undressed me. My wounds were wrapped, my clothing unbloodied. I dropped the sheet and looked back at her.

"*This* is a travesty," she said, showing me the inside of the pan. Black flecks caked the metal. "What'd you wash this with? Burnt chicken?"

"No, that was my dinner."

She *tsked* and tossed the pan back into the kitchen. It landed with a clatter. I winced again and groaned.

"Stay here," she said.

She pulled on her coat.

"Damn, and I was just gonna join a Broadway musical."

"We both know you can't dance."

I opened my mouth to reply, but she was already out the door. I lay back and stared at the ceiling for a while. Counted the things I knew. Cory was alive and wandering around. Ramirez was still dead. Someone had used me to bring a demon into the world, and I had no idea where it was. Someone had also tried to ice us. And the Aryan Bitch was still wandering around. That was a lot of someones and no answers.

It was a lot like when you're in line at Chipotle and they're out of guacamole, but no one can tell you when more's coming. Okay, not exactly like that. But someone was serving me brown guacamole, and I didn't like it.

I blinked at the thought and looked to my nightstand. A bottle of pills sat beside a glass of water and my wallet. I picked the bottle up, read the contents. Turns out Vicodin makes your brain a wet bowl of spaghetti. I cursed Ivy, but in a happy way, and closed my eyes, falling into my pillow.

Prison crept up on me like a bad friend.

We were eating lunch when I looked up from my bologna sandwich and swallowed. I looked at the other two men sitting with me, Richie and Dimes, and wondered if they'd think I was crazy. Dimly, I heard the other two discussing something about Tre, who somehow had just up and vanished. Doesn't matter, I thought. I cleared my throat.

"There's something in the walls."

My voice quavered. Fear wasn't a new thing in this place. You get used to it. But this was new fear. Had the stink of a fresh car.

Dimes snickered between bites. Richie stopped chewing and quirked an eyebrow. He looked me over. I knew Rich couldn't imagine me being afraid of too much short of a speeding freight train. Even then, he had some doubts as to the safety of the train. It was flattering, and uncomfortable, so the best of both worlds, really.

"Well, it's an old prison, man. Probably rats from way back," Rich said.

I nodded. "Yeah, man. You're probably right. I don't hear them anywhere else, though. It's something in the library. There's a door there. Behind the sixth shelf. Found it this morning. It's freaky as hell."

The "library", usually said with air quotes, was six shelves of books older than the warden, who was rumored to be older than Methuselah. It was shoved away in a corner of the prison, on one of the lower levels, and mostly forgotten. Still, it was a nice gig if you could get work there. Quiet, and safe. No one got shanked over a fifty-year-old copy of Time.

Dimes stopped chewing long enough to make a crack. "Maybe it's Richie's old lady. So horny she dug herself a tunnel, and now she's scratching to get in."

We ignored him.

"You tell the guards?" Richie asked.

I waved it away. "Nah. Why? So I can look like a bitch?"

"You just going to ignore it then?"

"Yeah, probably. They ain't getting' out."

"Well, at least we got that in common." Dimes said.

———

I t was an hour past lights-out, the only light on the level from the dimmed overhead banks. Richie muttered something in his sleep and rolled over. Every now and then, a guard walked by, flashing a light into the cell for a moment, then wandering past.

The bunk was bolted to the concrete wall, a washbasin toilet combo next to it, and a shelf with a small desk under it against the adjoining wall. For a moment, after the guard had passed, and the jingle of keys receded down the block, the prison was quiet enough to hear a soul slip free from its body, if you were listening.

Beside the bunk, in that preternatural stillness, came a faint sound. It was like a nail on stone—rasped across so gently, you could barely make it out. But it was there. It came once, twice, and again, louder

*each time. By the time it woke me, it was loud enough to sound like
metal on stone only inches from my face, on the other side of the wall.*

*I listened for a moment, lying still in the dark, heart racing. Each
scrape seemed to rasp across the inside of my eyes, and I imagined the
thing on the other side, digging its way to the freedom of my cell. I
pushed myself back, toward the edge of my bunk, and waited.*

*The sound went on for another minute, and then, the bright white of
a flashlight shone in. The sound ceased, and I stared at the wall, waiting
for it start again, even after the guard's footsteps had moved on.*

———

W e were eating breakfast when it came up again.
"Heard it in my cell last night," I said.
"What?" Richie asked.

"Those rats, man. I don't know if I can take it again. Spooky as shit.
You know, I might just open that door, and take care of business."

"With what? You gonna thump 'em with that spindly white cock?"
Dimes asked.

"Got a piece of wood I broke from one of the shelves. I can beat 'em
to a pulp with that."

"Shit, don't let Markham catch you with that."

A guard walked by the table, and we filled our mouths with breakfast until he passed.

"You guys wanna help?" I asked.

Dimes shook his head. "Got nothing against rats. The four-legged
kind, anyway."

I turned to Richie. "You?"

Richie shrugged. "Yeah, why not."

"Good on you, man. I'll get you a stick, too."

"Sure, when?"

"After lunch. Most of the guards get pretty slow in the afternoon. We
should have plenty of time to fuck around a bit."

"I'll be there."

We finished our meals, and left to go make plans, or blow off the rest of the morning.

―――――

Richie found me in the back of the library, pushing the last shelf in the row against the adjoining wall, forming an 'L' with the previous. Books littered the floor, and two sticks, about three and a half feet long leaned against the small desk in the corner. Richie picked one up and hefted it, then put it back when the sound of the shelves being moved stopped. I turned to him, and wiped my forehead with a kerchief I slipped back into a pocket.

"Help me reshelf these, and we can do some good ol' rodent huntin'."

Richie bent to grab a pile of books, and I did the same. We worked in silence for a while, moving books from the floor to the shelves. It was nice, the repetition. Almost like physical meditation.

When we were done, we leaned back on the shelves to catch our breath and took a look at the door. It was a normal-sized door, built from steel. There was a catch on the right side, where I assumed it could be pulled open, and a small hole above that, indicating a lock in place.

Small scratches marked this side of the door, and looking at them, I thought I saw a pattern, though the door was too old and worn from contact with the shelf and the books to make any sense of it. I leaned in to get a closer look, and Richie began to ask me what I saw there. Something grabbed my attention, and I raised a hand to quiet the inquiry.

Scratch. Scratch. Scratchscratch.

"You hear 'em, don't you?"

Richie nodded, and stepped away from the door.

"Imagine all day and night with that playing in your damn ears, man." I said. "Like the world's shittiest maraca band." I walked over to the sticks and picked them up, then handed one to Richie. "That shit needs to stop."

I went to the front of the library and looked around. The halls outside were empty, the sub-level quiet. We'd picked a good time to investigate. Most of the guards would be outside, or on the upper tiers, in the day rooms and the yard, while most of the inmates worked out, hung out, and bullshitted. I walked back to the door and pulled up the ring to the catch. Richie stood back a bit.

I pulled, the muscles in my arms cording as the door resisted, striations and veins bulging. The damn thing was heavier than a Buick. There was a sound of metal on metal, and a snap as the door broke free of it mooring of rust. It popped open, and rust puffed out in a fine red cloud. We took another step back and let the dust settle.

After a moment, when nothing else happened, Richie went to the door, and peered in the opening I had made. It was black beyond the threshold, and the air smelled stale and somehow wet, at the same time. From somewhere in the distance, that scratching sound came, deeper, and I thought of bone on stone. Richie stepped away from the door.

"What'd you see?" I asked.

Richie shook his head. "Nothin'. Too dark."

I walked over to the desk and opened a drawer with a key. From inside, I pulled out a cheap plastic flashlight. I tapped it twice, and flicked the switch, and it came on with a flicker resolving itself into a steady white circle of white.

"You really goin' in there?" Rich asked.

I nodded. "Yeah. Man's gotta get sleep. Had enough of these goddamn rats."

I shouldered past Richie and tugged the door open enough to let them to pass, then stepped into the passage. After a moment, Rich sighed, knowing he'd be labeled as a coward if he backed out now.

Inside, the light from my flashlight showed the walls were rough concrete, and a pair of stairs winding downwards. Cobwebs clung to the ceiling and stirred in wispy waves from the fresh air that had been let into the passage. I started forward, down the stairs, and Richie followed.

The stairs were worn smooth with age. They were damp here and there with moisture seeping from the walls and dripping occasionally *from the ceiling. The air was colder in the passage too, and I shivered involuntarily. A gust of air from further down blew upwards, and the smell of rot and mildew came stronger. I pushed forward, intent on my destination.*

After a while, the stairs grew steeper and wetter, the stone all dark and slick at that point. We chose their footing a bit more carefully as we went. Something dark and black and warm went scurrying by, and Richie let out a little yelp. I lashed out with my stick, and there was a dull thud, and a squeak.

"Gotcha, you fucker!" I stepped over the body, and saw the remains in the ambient light from the flashlight. It was a rat, about two feet long, with deep black fur, and a naked tail curled into a loop. It lay on its side, blood pooling around its head, eyes staring out into the dark. I stepped over it, and we continued.

Eventually, the stairs ended, and the passage leveled out. We followed it a bit further, the stench of rot, and what had to be wet fur, getting stronger all the time. Then, the passage ended, and we found themselves in an open cavern, stalactites and stalagmites growing from the ceiling and floor. In an open space, something huge and pale and fleshy lay, while what looked like hundreds of rats nursed from it.

There was another thud from behind me, and it took me a moment to tear my eyes away from the pale flesh of the queen rat to look back at Richie. What I got instead was the sight of Markham standing over Richie with a heavy-duty guard's flashlight, the black barrel wet with blood. He looked up at me.

"Feed the Queen, boy." He gestured at Rich's body. I didn't move, and Markham stepped closer, his voice still laconic, but his posture aggressive. "Feed her or be food."

I made my decision. I knelt and picked up Rich. I carried the body over to the pale thing on the floor, careful not to step on any of the dark moving objects. I looked up for a moment, and saw a chute leading from the ceiling, and near the bottom, a pile of human bones. Skulls, femurs, and ribs littered the ground.

"You didn't think we actually buried you fuckers, did you?"
Markham asked from behind him.

I moved to the front of the pale beast on the floor and set Rich's body
down. The thing stirred, and a vast black eye opened. It regarded me,
and I was sure for an instant I could feel someone, or something, rifling
through his mind like a filing cabinet. Then it was gone, and the gaze
turned on Rich's body.

One by one, the smaller rats filed to it, and carefully, began to rip
chunks of flesh away. I was thankful m friend was probably already
dead. As I watched, the file of rats began to drop the food into the pale
beast's open mouth, which chewed each piece, and opened for another.

My stomach threatened to rebel, and I felt a hand on my shoulder.

"Good job, boy. I think we've got a new job assignment for you." The
hand clapped me on the back, and then turned me back toward the
staircase. After only a moment of hesitation, I began to walk.

T hat night, the scratching came again, but it was brief. When I
woke in the morning, there was something in my sink. It looked
like an ear.

I kept my eyes shut for a minute longer. I'd had a lot of weird
dreams. A lot of weird experiences in my time chained to the
demons, but this was a new one.

Christ, Vicodin dreams are wild, I thought.

When I opened them again, light had slid across the room,
marking it somewhere near noon. I still ached, but I was thinking
clearer. I made my way to the bathroom, stumbling only a couple
times, and banging my ribs once. I took deep breaths, the pain
coming in waves. When it subsided, I did my business and came
back.

Ivy had silently set the kitchen table, and a spread waited for us.
Take-out bags sat in a row on the counter. If there's such a thing as

Heaven on earth, it's surely built from Italian food. I'd seriously considered having my coffin built from their garlic bread. You know, in case I woke up as a focaccia-craving zombie. I loved that place.

"You're the best cook," I said.

She ushered me to a chair, then took one herself. I was glad for the help. Even the short trip down the hall had taken a lot out of me. The room smelled of garlic and cream and marinara, tin plates heaped and steaming with bread and pasta and vegetables. I dug in, dropping enough on my plate to feed a small army. The only way I could be happier is if someone stabbed me to death with a slice of pizza for dessert.

For a time, the only sounds between us were the simple pleasure of good food and the chirp of birds and susurrus of traffic outside. When we finished, we pushed back, groaning. My ribs still ached, but it was a companionable one from overstuffing myself.

Still we didn't speak, sipping wine and just enjoying each others' company. The drink made my head fuzzy, and I wandered over to my bed, laying back. Ivy came to stand over me, a slight frown furrowing her forehead.

"Sit up," she ordered.

I did, groaning a little. She knelt in front of me and opened my shirt. Her hands explored my side and chest, her touch light and gentle. It still drew a slight hiss of pain from me.

"Sorry," she murmured.

Her fingers traced an old scar, and she shook her head a little.

"Why do you do it, Jack?"

I shrugged, the motion making me sway, and she held on for a moment. "Someone's got to."

"I think you're a better man than you let on."

I realized how close she was sitting, smelled shea butter and coconut, and something citrusy—probably her perfume.

Her touch increased in pressure, the heat in her fingers like embers. She lifted her chin to look at me. Her lips were so close.

She leaned in, brushed them against mine, eyes half-lidded. Her hands moved from my ribs to my back, slender fingers splayed across my shoulder blades.

She pulled me in for a kiss. I'd imagined it, and suddenly even that felt inadequate. Llyrial kept his mouth shut, and it made something deep in me stir. This was more than an infatuation. I'd denied it so long that when it came, it was like sun on the brink of spring. She tasted of garlic and onion, and I didn't care. I felt heat, smelled smoke. I opened my eyes and drew back.

"You smell smoke?" I asked.

"Jack," she whispered. "No."

I looked out the window. A thin gray streamer billowed past. Annoyance warred with appreciation at the universe's ability to fuck with me. I sighed. "No, it's definitely smoke."

She opened her eyes, raised an eyebrow. A slight smile curled the corners of her lips. "This is a terrible time to have a stroke," she said.

Something *plinked* through my kitchen window. I didn't see what it was. The second it landed, flames burst from the source, engulfing my kitchen and the remains of our meal. Smoke clouded the room, and I slid from the bed, drawing Ivy down with me to the floor.

"Fuck," I cursed. The place was going up far faster than I'd give a normal fire. "We're gonna have to jump," I said.

Flames crackled, the heat enough to make my skin ache.

"Are you out of your goddamn mind? Contrary to popular belief, I don't own a broom," she said.

"What?" I looked at her.

"Witches don't fly."

I nodded absently, looking for an exit. There was another way, but it was gonna hurt like a bastard. More than I already hurt, so like two bastards.

"Just a second," I said.

"Jack, what are you—" her sentence cut off in a scream as a

section of the kitchen collapsed, sending sparks and flaming debris raining our way.

I grabbed Ivy up, smelled roasting hair, felt the sharp pain of a burn, and decided I didn't want to know. I had never been that hairy, but I was fond of the ones I did have.

"Hang on," I said.

She wrapped her arms around my neck. I held her in mine, and then I ran toward the broken window. Whoever had set Cory free, and chucked the firestarter in had done me a favor. There was very little glass in my way.

I called on Regnos, and the demon answered with glee. I felt my skin harden; my muscles become somehow *more.* I put on speed as another chunk of ceiling rained down, nearly braining me. Ivy held tight, making a low sound in her throat.

I slammed into the sill and it shattered under the force and weight of the impact. And then we were falling. I'm not a fan of heights at the best of times, so this was easily categorized into my top ten nightmares of all-time. Add a clown riding James Woods like a pony, and I would've needed new pants.

Ivy's murmur became a series of *NOs* as we fell. I wrapped myself around her and turned my back to the ground.

It felt like we fell for an eternity. It felt like we fell in no time at all.

And then I slammed into the pavement like a chicken carcass tossed off a roof. I felt something re-break. Regnos subsumed the pain for a moment, then faded as my head slammed into the asphalt. It bounced once, and the world winked out for a moment.

Then Ivy was straddling me, slapping me awake.

"Jack! Jack! Wake the fuck up!"

I smiled up at her, and she stopped slapping me.

"What's so goddamn funny, Nyx?" She asked.

"The fact that I would've been really happy with this position ten minutes ago."

She snorted, and all the stress seemed to leave her. She slumped over, laying her head on my chest. Something inside me screamed in agony. Something else was pumping blood like a broken Super Soaker. But it didn't matter for the moment. We were safe.

13

Firemen tend to ask very few questions while there's a fire. It's almost like their job is to put it out. We used the opportunity to slink away, Ivy supporting me through a back alley until we made it out the other side. Once on a main street, she flagged down a cab and got us back to her place, the driver agreeing we didn't exist in exchange for Ivy's Rolex.

We were both exhausted and covered in soot. Pain flared in every part of me, and my left leg kept going numb. I didn't like what that meant. I'd likely slipped a disc at best. At worst, I'd snapped a vertebra. In addition, I kept wanting to nap. Everything looked like a bed, and it felt like my head was wrapped in six layers of cotton.

I hobbled over to her couch, the good one, and ruined it for sure this time. It was a sign we'd both been through hell when the most I got was a half-hearted glare. She rummaged around the kitchen for a while, pulling things from mason jars and tossing them into a pot on the stove.

The smell filling the air was indescribable. Strike that. It smelled like someone had started baking a turkey, and halfway through, decided it would be tastier if they shoved an octopus inside it. Like some sort of ichthyological travesty. She worked silently, finishing up with a blue puff of smoke she waved away, then bustled over to me with a glass holding something the color of puke and half as attractive. I shied back involuntarily.

"Drink this," she said.

I eyed it. "I seem to remember that not working out so well for Alice."

"Drink this or take it rectally."

I sniffed it, drew back at the way the scent smacked me in the face. "I'll tell you what. I'll just die here, and you can use my body to freshen up the place."

"Fine, I'll get the tubing."

"Shit, okay, okay." I took the glass from her and slammed the contents. It had the consistency of kombucha but tasted light and airy, like rose petals. The second it hit my system, a warmth suffused my limbs, and I felt better.

"What the hell was that?"

"About ten thousand dollars."

"Holy shit."

"And the couch is another three."

Pain fled my body, and I felt better than I had in a week. I looked at the glass.

"Was that a healing potion? Like wizards make?"

"Wizards make fire and weird giraffe-monkey hybrids. That was my emergency potion. Fixes what ails you."

She flopped onto the couch next to me, leaned on my shoulder. I set the glass down and sat back.

"Giraffe-monkey?" I asked.

"Guy in Hoboken. Don't ask."

Silence passed between us for a few more minutes.

"Ten thou?" I asked.

Her only answer was a snore. I leaned back, and she snuggled into my chest. I wondered how I was going to pay back these debts I'd been accruing. I didn't like owing anyone. Debt was a sword of Damocles, hanging by a thread made of nickels and dimes.

I pushed it to the back of my mind. I'd worry about it later if I made it through this. Ivy's potion had gone a long way toward keeping me in the game. The pain gone, my brain told me I was tired. I listened. Lassitude filled my limbs and I closed my eyes.

———

I stood before the Maze again. A whole flood of memory came rushing in, threatening to drown me. I walled it off, inspected my surroundings. Gray walls rose above, stretching ten, fifteen feet. They were uniform and seamless, the entrance before me leading a short way to a blank wall and a t-intersection. I looked up. Obsidian floated in a sky the color of a bruise. Some housed manors of the same rock. Spires and minarets made silhouettes against the purple-black. Others were great Brutalist works—featureless cubes with arrow slits for windows. I knew the Dukes of Hell reigned there and hoped to avoid their attention.

This particular rock was different. It held only the Maze. And whatever lived there.

I turned my focus back. I'd tried scaling the walls once, to get the lay of the land. There's something there, above the top of the walls—something alien. I don't remember a lot. A presence, huge and crushing. The regard of an unfathomable mind. It left me puking my guts out. I didn't do it again.

A voice caught my ear, from somewhere ahead. I cursed under my breath.

"Jack," it said.

I knew Ramirez when I heard him. I'd spent hours listening to the man lecture about the soul, binding, and the value of a good bourbon-cigar coupling.

"Hey!" I shouted. "How 'bout you come out. We can sit down, have a nice... okay, not a picnic, but something."

"Jack!" This, more insistent.

I looked around. I knew this was a dream. Or hoped it was. If something planned on dropping me back here on a regular basis when I slept, I'd have to give serious thought to taking up a meth habit.

The call again, this time strident, breaking. My insides curled up, tried to play dead. Tried to remind me of the pain I'd carried for so long, of the sorrow. It wanted to drag me under that wave of memory again, force me to suck its gray water in, fill my guts and lungs with hurt. I ignored it and took a breath.

"Fuck me," I whispered.

I reached out, felt Llyrial and Regnos. Felt the dark something that was Xiphos, slumbering. They waited beneath the surface, quiescent but eager. I was as ready as I'd ever be. I stepped into the Maze.

The Maze is a test. Rather, it's the Final Test. The reason there are very few demonites is because you pass, or you don't, and if you don't, well, there's no body to clean up. Hell isn't wasteful. Ramirez told me a story once, about a kid form Peoria. Straight-A student, well-behaved. He stepped into the Maze, and just... vanished. About three weeks later, a woman in Texas opened her fridge to find her aspic filled with hair and eyes.

I made my way carefully through twisting passages, the walls impassive. Left and right and right and left and sometimes counter-clockwise to move forward. The Maze was never the same twice, so no one demonite could tell another the easy way through. Couple that with the challenges at every junction, and each person who passed through had a unique experience. And by unique, I mean a shitty time at the ol' Circle-K.

I'd expect nothing less of something anchored in Hell, anyway.

I came on the first intersection, paths branching out in four directions. They'd been designed as mini arenas, each about twenty feet square, enough room to kill or be killed.

The walls rippled, the surfaces becoming liquid. Five devourers slipped from the portals, blackened half-skulls drinking in the light. They had no eyes, just a nose and a mouth filled with razor teeth. Their skin was uniform gray tending to black at the ends of their too-long limbs.

They sniffed the air, turned toward me.

"Ah, fellas. I've already done this," I said, backing up.

I knew I'd have to fight, regardless. The things in the Maze, once free from their prisons, gave chase until one of you was dead.

I felt a pang of disappointment from Llyrial as the devourers advanced, and I nodded in sympathy.

"Always a flesh-eater, never a succubus," I said, though God only knew if you could actually bang one to submission.

Not a pleasant thought either way. Succubi eat souls. It's bone or be boned. I winced at the thought of the friction burns and called on Regnos. She came with a roar of joy. Strong here. I felt strength enter my limbs, my skin hardening.

The first of the devourers came at me, and I lowered my shoulder, checked it under the jaw with a rising elbow. The thing's skull exploded in a puff of ash, and I spun into a backfist, hammering my knuckles into its partner. The skull burst there, too.

The third got a talon into me and ripped a gouge down my triceps. I ignored the flare of pain and the hot blood pouring down my arm and grabbed it by the head, snapping its neck.

Four and five came on as a team, one leaping on me and bearing me to the ground while the other went for my groin. I lashed out with a boot, smashing its teeth down its throat. No Nyx sausage for you, bubba. It staggered back and collapsed.

That left number five, who was doing its level best to pin me to the floor of the Maze by slamming six-inch claws through my shoulder. I screamed as snapping teeth came close to my throat and punched upward with both fists. They shattered the thing's sternum and tore through the skin like it was tissue paper. It too crumbled to dust, leaving me alone and bleeding in the dirt.

I worked my way up. I tried to push Regnos away, but she was *clinging, and once I had my feet, I found myself charging toward the next intersection. I tried to throw myself at a wall, anything to stop the runaway rage beast, but too late, and I stumbled into the arena.*

The wall rippled, and a thing built like a truck and over seven feet stepped out, a massive blade over its shoulder. Black horns rose above its head, pointed like a bull's. Its face was half-human, half-shark, and it grinned when it saw me.

"Demonite," it said in hellspeak.

Regnos roared. I was just barely in control at this point, and she knew it. She threw us at the cacodemon, and I managed to twist just in time as it lowered the blade, intending to spit me on it.

I rolled in the dust, spitting dirt as I found my feet.

"Great idea," I said. "Challenge the demon equivalent of Rowdy Roddy Piper."

The cacodemon moved in, blade swinging in a decapitating blow. I slipped under it and threw two rabbit punches at its midsection. They had the same effect as a child kicking a Buick.

It growled and reversed its swing. I ducked under the blade, coming inside the demon's guard.

"Okay, you lunatic. Help me out here," I said, and grabbed its elbow.

Regnos replied with a wild cackle of laughter and lent me more strength. I bent the demon's arm the wrong way and was rewarded with the sound of bones snapping. I made another mental note to ask Regnos someday why she liked doing that. The blade fell from nerveless fingers, and I snatched it from the dirt as the cacodemon howled in pain.

I scooped up the sword and hefted it. Too heavy to swing, even with Regnos. I watched as the cacodemon recovered. We circled one another for a moment. Its eyes narrowed, and it spat a word.

"Tainted."

It charged, and I did the bravest thing I knew. I held the big knife out and hid behind it. The cacodemon tried to turn its run into a skid as I set myself, but it was too late, and it impaled itself, saving me some work. Its weight dragged the weapon from my hands, and I collapsed to the ground with a sigh of relief.

For a moment, it felt as if Regnos was going to challenge me for control again. I fought her back, hammering on her will with my own bolstered by anger. Finally, she receded.

My hands were shaking, and I raised them to wipe the sweat from my eyes. The skin was a dull red, and pebbled, the nails black and pointed.

Tainted.

I understood, then. I'd let the demon take too much, and we'd nearly become the same.

"Jack!"

I didn't have time to worry about it. I forced myself to my feet and made my way deeper into the Maze.

———

C rows lined the walls of the intersection. Ramirez sat in the dirt there. My heart clenched, and for a moment, I couldn't speak. I hadn't had the best track record with parents, so the old man had been my substitute. I still felt the pain of his death.

Still, this felt like a trick: 'Hey, your pops is back from the dead! Come give daddy a hug!'

I stood just outside. He looked up, eyes black as coal.

"Seven," he said. "Seven crows. Do you remember?"

I thought on our lessons. There was a rhyme he was fond of.

"One for sorrow,

Two for mirth

Three for a funeral,

Four for birth

Five for heaven

Six for hell

Seven for the devil, his own self," I said.

Somewhere deeper in the Maze, something roared, as if it had been wounded.

"Go now," Ramirez said.

That roar again, like the tearing of the world.

"GO."

The dream shattered.

———

I woke to Ivy standing over me with a cup of coffee and a scowl.

"That couch is completely fucked."

I sat up and looked, still trying to shake the cobwebs of the dream. The ivory fabric had been stained with black and red. My shoulder and arm ached. I winced and took the coffee from her. She sat next to me.

"I don't even want to know how you managed to bleed in your sleep. And your hands—" she ended it with a scoff.

"It's a knack."

"Mm-hmm. Drink your coffee, Edward Demon Hands."

Ivy'd done enough, and I'd done enough to her wallet, so the least I could do was make breakfast. Flapjacks du Jack. I could've just kept it 'flapjacks', but I'm fancy like that. The apartment smelled of warmed syrup and fried dough, and we sat before a stack of pancakes and a plate of bacon. It didn't take long for us to make short work of the meal.

When we'd finished, we sipped our coffee. Mine, hot and black. Hers, light and sweet. If I were a more poetic man, I'd find something romantic in that. Or maybe a crasser man. As it was, I was too full of pancakes.

"Tell me about the dream. Or whatever the hell it was."

I looked over at her wall of movie posters. Pinhead stared back at me; the puzzle box cupped in his hands. I winced involuntarily. Hell has high priests, but they don't usually waste time with speech or theatrics. The Maze flashed into my mind again, and I sighed. I told her everything that had happened, and the poem Ramirez had been speaking.

"Why were his eyes black?" She asked.

I shrugged, showed her my hands. They still hadn't changed back.

"Tainted," I said. "Happens when you let the demon take too much control, or for too long. Most cases revert after a while, but some never do. And anytime you call on a demon in Hell, it's stronger. That's why the Maze. It teaches us to retain control. I got sloppy."

"And the rhyme?"

I shrugged. "I'm more concerned with how I got sucked back to Hell in the first place. I need to find someone else with experience in that field. Preferably someone with a familiarity with Enochian. I don't know what else they might have tattooed into Praedolor's circle."

She raised an eyebrow. "You can't read it all?"

"I uh, wasn't the best student."

"So what you're telling me is if it was Latin—"

"Yes, I'd know how to ask for the bathroom."

"And this didn't occur to you before, why?"

"You know, explosions, stabbings, getting the piss kicked out of me. Tends to knock some things right out of your head."

"Yeah, I've been meaning to talk to you about that. How many times did you say you've been concussed?"

"I don't remember."

"Funny. You're funny. Also, you don't have an apartment anymore."

"Yeah, that's a problem. I hate sleeping in alleys. People pee on me."

Her lips made a line for a moment. "You can stay here."

I opened my mouth to protest. It was obvious there was a target on my back. I didn't want her to get hurt. Of all the people and things I couldn't muster empathy for, Ivy wasn't one. She was the best friend I'd ever made. Sure, maybe it was a little chauvinist. But more, I just wanted my friends safe. I'd only made a few in my life, and most had gone the way of the dodo.

She frowned, as if reading my mind. "Don't start that chivalrous bullshit with me. I already know how deep we are. Besides, they tried to kill me, too. So. You will stay here, and you will not hold things back like an idiot. Am I clear?"

I nodded.

"And you will replace my couch," she added.

I groaned. "That's like a hundred bucks."

"Try three grand, mister."

"I have trouble with large numbers."

"You're gonna have trouble with my foot in your ass. Now tell me where we can find your expert."

I downed the rest of my coffee. I'd been dreading this since someone saddled me with Praedolor.

"The Enclave."

"Ooh, mysterious," she said.

"Annoying," I replied. "You know how rich people like to shit everything up in favor of themselves?"

"Yeah…"

"Well, these are rich assholes with demons at their beck and call."

"Fan-fucking-tastic. Just remember what ol' Jack Burton does when the earth quakes, and the poison arrows fall from the sky, and the pillars of Heaven shake. Yeah, Jack Burton just looks that big ol' storm right square in the eye and he says, "Give me your best shot, pal. I can take it."

"Who the fuck's Jack Burton?"

"Big Trouble in Little China?"

"Never seen it."

She sputtered for a moment.

"We'll fix that," she promised. "Now, how do we find this Enclave?"

"Easy enough. Cigar club on Front."

"Ah, hiding in plain sight. Clever."

"Sure, what do snakes have to fear, anyway?"

"The mongoose."

I gave her a blank look.

"Oh, come on! Rikki Tikki Tavi?

I shook my head and put my dishes in the sink. It was gonna be a long day.

I vy checked the half-ass bandage job I'd done on my arm and shoulder, then cleaned the wounds and put new dressings on them. It'd have to do. Neither of us had the ingredients for her fancy potion laying around, and I certainly didn't have ten grand in the couch cushions. I added the cost to a mental tally before we left. At the rate I was going, I'd owe her for the next hundred years. Assuming I lived past the rest of the week.

She led us to a BMW in the parking garage.

"What happened to the Mercedes?"

"Needed a change of scenery."

"How much did you say you make a year?"

"Enough," she said, and put the car into gear.

We made good time through weekend streets that hadn't quite woken yet. We used it to not talk about what had almost happened at my apartment. Like I'd said. Ivy was one of my closest and oldest friends. Like a flower growing too close to a weed, you can't just rip the roots out and expect it to survive. There were things tangled there. I knew we'd eventually have to broach the subject, but when someone's trying to fit your head for a hatbox, you have more pressing matters.

The cigar club was a little place tucked into a strip mall, between a coin-op laundry and a sandwich shop that had definitely not been shut down three times for food poisoning, or so the sign in their window said. A plaque above the tinted glass door and windows marked the club out as Castro's. Very imaginative. Much funny. A bell went off deeper in the building as we entered.

The front room was a lushly appointed affair. Overstuffed armchairs, hardwood end tables, humidors, and a bar against one wall. Everything was done in leather, hardwood, and that particular green you only see in clubs like this or billiard halls. This was the sort of place people with money came to get away from people without it, and it reeked of Cohibas and disdain.

A couple of patrons sat in the chairs, puffing away, the air exchange a gentle hum. Whatever was on the roof was quiet and powerful. Like the people who ran this place. A woman stood behind the bar, tattoos showing beneath the rolled-up sleeves of her white button-up marking her as both a lust and delusion bearer. Her hair was cropped short on the sides and long on top, jet-black. She smiled as we approached, appraising Ivy.

People think of witches as haggard old women crouched over cauldrons, cackling and warty. Ivy was none of those things. A complexion smooth and clear enough to bathe in. Hair twisted into braids complementing her heart-shaped face. Eyes the color of teak, flecked with gold. She'd stop a normal man or woman's heart on her worst day.

In addition, the nature of her business meant she had to deal with people on a regular basis, which made her a natural at the things I was terrible at, namely making friends and not sticking out like a blood-stained hammer in a tea set. I figured it was a better idea she talk to the woman.

I stared at the door in the back of the room marked EMPLOYEES ONLY and looked to her. Ivy frowned and shook her head slightly, which was Ivy telepathy for *if you kick that door in, I'll turn you into a newt.* She could do it, too.

She sidled up to the bar and I leaned against it, keeping my eye on the room. She set her elbows on the wood, striking up a conversation. The women spoke in quiet tones, punctuated by the occasional laugh. The men in the room took no notice, except to maybe glance over at me in curiosity. It wasn't every day someone like me wandered into a place that looked like this. I was disheveled at best at this point. I ignored the whole affair. If it'd been meant for my ears, they would've been speaking to me.

Finally, Ivy straightened.

"C'mon," she said.

She tucked a small white business card into her breast pocket. I hurried to catch up.

"Nicely done," I said as we approached the door.

Ivy shrugged. "I played the pity angle."

"And she believed that?"

"I mean, look at you."

I looked down. Ivy had loaned me a set of clean clothing, but it was all a bit baggy. I assumed it was an ex's. We've all got those sorts of things laying around. Baggage from past lives. Or at least, I had, until someone set the heaviest of mine free. In addition, I was still a bit grimy. Ash and blood are hard to get completely out.

I shrugged. "Fair enough."

The door buzzed, followed by the click of the lock. I tugged it open, and we stepped through. The next room was much like the other, with the addition of shelves and shelves of books. Two men and a woman sat in armchairs before a conjured fire. The oldest, Schopen, had to be about eighty. He was pale, skin nearly translucent. Blue veins spidered across his bald pate. The other, Felix, was a stocky Latino man in his forties. The last, Shen, was Asian, likely in her thirties. Tattoos crawled across every inch of exposed flesh, ending at their necks and wrists.

I knew of them, but until now never had a reason to visit. Like anytime you finally see someone in person, there are details you miss out. I did some mental math, and unless they'd managed to make binding circles smaller, each of these people commanded at least six demons. In addition, every inch of the room and their clothing screamed money like a rabid Scrooge McDuck. These were people who not only had luxury but had *access.*

The woman gestured to a set of chairs placed across from them.

"Mr. Nyx. Ms. Sosye. Have a seat."

We settled in, the chair nearly swallowing me. I struggled to sit upright. Shen raised an eyebrow, and Felix blew a soft snort of amusement. Ivy glared at me.

"Look, they're very squishy," I said.

"I understand you need our help, Mr. Nyx," Schopen said, interrupting me.

"Clearly," Ivy muttered.

"As it were," the old man continued, ignoring the both of us, "we've been monitoring your little… situation."

I narrowed my eyes in suspicion. "Why?"

"You can't fart in this town without getting our attention, Mr. Nyx," Shen said. "And in this case, you've entirely shit the bed."

Felix leaned forward and placed a small black object on the table between us.

"Recognize this?" He asked.

Ivy picked it up, rubbed it between her fingers. A scowl crossed her features. "This is one of mine."

She tossed it to me. I caught it and looked closely. One of her talisman coins. The symbols had been altered. I didn't know what they meant, but I knew the result.

"They change these marks here, and pump it with a little magic, and *boom*, firestarter," I said.

Schopen nodded. "Between Cagliostro and the cult, I suspect one of you has made a powerful enemy. Tell me, did you ever find the soul that escaped its confinement?"

"Cory?" I asked. "No, he wouldn't—" then I remembered he'd killed Ramirez. "Are you saying he did this?"

Shen spread her hands. "We don't know. But we think it's likely he's involved."

"And the demon?"

"Ah, Praedolor," Felix said. "That was regrettable. Show us the markings."

I stood and unbuttoned my shirt, pulling it down. There was silence in the room for a moment. I looked at Ivy. She had a slight smile quirking the corner of her mouth. I frowned at her. She mouthed *bow chicka bow wow* at me.

"You may redress, Mr. Nyx."

I buttoned up and sat. "Well?"

"The circle is no different than any other binding circle, regardless of the crudeness. Whatever your other troubles may be, this is not the cause."

Well shit, dead-end.

"So, what can we do?"

"We suggest you find this Cory. And you subdue the demon before it causes more carnage."

"And how am I supposed to do that? And why haven't you if you know so much?"

Shen spoke up. "We're believers in the idea that the Lord helps those who help themselves."

"So, you're useless," I said.

"Jack…" Ivy warned.

"No, I come here for help, and these assholes sit in their patent leather chairs and fellate each other over how powerful they are."

Regnos growled in my chest.

"TAINTED," the old man's voice boomed, and I felt a sudden weight press me into the chair.

I struggled for a moment, Regnos thrashing against the bonds. Llyrial joined in, and the air grew thick. Sweat sprung from Schopen's forehead. Then the pressure doubled, tripled, and pain flared through my limbs. Regnos and Llyrial retreated with a whimper.

Finally, the pressure retreated. I looked at them. "You don't know anything, do you?"

Shen spoke up. "Leave, Mr. Nyx. Our generosity wears thin."

I opened my mouth to protest, but Ivy was already pulling me from the chair. We made our way from the room in silence, the lock clicking behind us. It was still early, the morning turning bright.

"Where to?" Ivy asked.

Gabriel. The name popped into my head like a curse. She was the reason I'd gone to prison. Well, that, and the robbery. But Gabriel had been the catalyst. I'd been young, thought I'd do anything for love. Thought that's what love was. It had gone wrong, as things like that tend to. I still had a smoking hole in my heart from the whole affair.

"Jack?" Ivy asked.

I blinked. "I've got to talk to an ex."

She raised an eyebrow.

"Nothing for you to worry about."

"We're not even dating."

"I know. I just wanted to clarify. But if anyone might know where that kid is, it's her."

"What're you going to do?"

"Track her down. If Cory's out there, she'll know where he is."

"Need help?"

I shook my head. "Gabriel's unpredictable at the best of times. And she's... she's a Divine."

"You were in bed with an angel?"

"I didn't know. And angel is a... loaded term. She's more of a freelancer."

"Ah. Hey, there's a phone in my bag. I want you to take it."

I groaned, and she smacked me playfully in the back of the head.

"Difference between being idiosyncratic and being smart. Be smart, Jack," she said.

"Fine, I'll take the distraction box if it'll make you happy."

"It will. You wouldn't like me when I'm angry."

"Or hungry."

"Spoken like a man who wants to eat from a tube."

I yawned loud and long. Sleep crowded in like a fat guy on the subway, pushing everything else out of my head.

"Sure. But first, a nap."

We made our way back to the apartment, and Ivy climbed into the couch beside me and snuggled into my side. The warmth from her concoction had finally subsided, and they were low-key aching, but not screaming. My brain tried to tangle up my feelings. I didn't have time for it and pushed them aside. We fell asleep like that for a while.

I woke in the small hours. Ivy had shifted and slept at a weird angle. Part of me wanted to wake her. Part of me didn't feel like talking just yet. I grabbed my stuff, digging the phone out of Ivy's bag. I crept out and made my way downtown to the ruins of my apartment. The building was a blackened soggy shell. I stood outside, listening to the still-dripping timbers. I couldn't bring myself to feel completely disconnected. It wasn't much, but it was mine, for a time. I picked my way over a tangle of timber and wet fabric to where my bed had been. The box underneath it was still there, only slightly blackened.

I pressed my palm to the lid, and it clicked softly. Inside, a Sig Sauer lay nestled in packing foam. I took it, and the rune-tipped bullets out, and shoved it into my jacket. I looked the rest of the mess over, decided there wasn't anything in there worth saving, and moved on.

14

You ever had one of those days? You know the kind—coffee grounds in the coffee, burnt toast, cat gets out—people won't stay dead. That's the kind of day I was having. I'd had to lean on a few contacts, but they'd finally given me the name of a man who might lead me to Gabriel. I had stalked the man to a local pub, the Broken Oar, a dive just off the riverside. It smelled of algae and fish—something rotted. I watched him go in and stood in a doorway across from the entrance.

I stepped deeper into the shadow of the doorway, shoving my hands into my pockets. I shifted uncomfortably, the pistol in its docker's clutch digging into my armpit. I hated it. I hated the weight, the smell. The way it kicked, like something belligerent, the feel cold and dead in my hand.

I had always felt that way about guns, I guess. They weren't cool, or pretty, or sleek or sexy. They were cold steel and rubber, oiled spring and mechanism, and they had one purpose. To make a hole as large as possible in something living.

Still—I reached inside the jacket and snapped the safety strap off the clutch, letting the pistol's weight fall into my hand. The metal was cold—colder than metal usually is. I suspected it was the runes on the rounds. They practically spoke the need to take a life.

I pulled it out, grabbing the slide and pulling it back as quietly as possible. There was a click—oiled and smooth—from the mechanism as it lifted a shell into place and secured it in the chamber.

I looked at the gun for a moment—it was black, plain with Pachmayr grips. Not fancy. Definitely effective.

I shoved it deep in my jacket pocket at the end of my fist. Better safe than sorry, and all that shit.

———

I was almost out of patience. I told myself it was only another hour and blew on my hands for the fortieth time that night to warm them. I had given up on the pistol for the time being, knowing if I kept squeezing it in that death-grip, only one of two things would happen—I would lose the circulation and flexibility in my fingers, or I would shoot myself in the foot.

I hated this—these guys that would do anything for a buck. Sure, I was one of them. But there were lines. The door across the street opened, spilling light and sound onto the street. I saw the man exit, a woman on his arm. She was drunk. I groaned inwardly, knowing what was next. First the drinking, then the sex—something that could only end badly. If you didn't know the demons, they could use you up, leave you limp.

I watched as they turned the corner into an alley, and slipped my hand back around the pistol, my finger resting on the trigger guard. I stepped from the doorway and followed, stopping at the corner, and peeping around. The smell of rot was strong, and I sucked in a breath of fresh air before I stepped in, the pistol out and ready. In the dark at the back of the alley I could hear heavy breathing and caught the smell of alcohol on the breeze.

There were the sounds of moaning, and a zipper. Then,

laughter. I felt the growl rise in the Vessel's throat even before I heard it, the vibration rising in the air like a hum. I popped out from my hiding place, the pistol forward.

He spun, and I snapped the pistol down, at his solar plexus, raising the barrel even as he launched himself at me. I squeezed the trigger and the air reverberated with a boom. The Vessel snapped back in midair, crumpling heap on the stones.

The Vessel twitched.

I watched as he raised himself from the ground, his face breaking into a grin as he looked first at the wound, then at me. Somewhere in the background, a woman screamed.

He staggered toward me at first, still weak from the damage I'd done him. I put my hand on his chest, a little disconcerted. It's rare that the runes etched into the soft lead of the hollow tip don't stop someone. He looked up, and his arms followed suit, his hands wrapping around my neck. His face had begun to split, and behind it I could see the thing that lived there.

Shit, I thought. Getting slow, old man.

My breath had begun to come in ragged wisps, and darkness bloomed in my vision. I got the gun up and the air shook again. I smelled cordite and ozone. The demonite staggered back, the grin turning to a snarl—he was getting pissed, and I had better do something.

I extended my hand, feeling the thrum in the air. I saw the runes in my eye, and even as the thing leaped at me, its flesh falling away, fingers extending to talons, flesh scaling and teeth elongating to fangs, I unleashed Regnos to speak the Word.

It was a trick I'd only used a couple of times. Magic wasn't my bag for the most part, and tapping into demonic magic was dangerous on a good day. Think insta-fried chicken if you get it wrong.

My bones thrummed, my still-healing wounds sending up an ache. The Word shattered the air, hammering the thing back in mid-leap and ramming it against the brick wall of the pub.

The holes in its chest glowed, smoke and ichor pouring out. The Vessel screamed and tore at his chest Its claws made the wound worse. In a matter of seconds, he was engulfed in blue flame licking at his chest, and in a minute, nothing more was left than a pile of soft tissue and ash.

I let out a long sigh, looking around. No one had popped their head into the alley, or if they did, they decided against sticking around long. I stooped to pick up the spent shells, the last of the magic trickling out into my palm as I cradled them.

I wondered how this was going to get me any closer to Gabriel, or if the people I'd spoken to were just setting me up. I looked at the remains of the man and frowned. Taint was a hazard, but this seemed almost as if he'd never had control. Regardless, now I had a corpse I couldn't question. Well, I could. It'd just be weird.

The screaming woman had long gone, probably run out after the second shot. Good. That meant she'd go home, shower, and forget. The human mind can be a tidy little housekeeper, something I'm more than glad for. The only thing that really disappointed me were the shells. They were hard to make, hard to find, and the fact I had wasted this many on something that should never have been walking around in the first place irritated me.

I looked around, slipped the pistol back into the docker's clutch, and pocketed the shell casings. One more look, and I walked back to the body. A good kick, and I scattered the ashes, the wind snatching them and swirling them toward the sky.

Another damn dead end. I called Ivy and let her know this was going to take longer than I'd expected. She texted me her credit card and I hunkered down in a motel on the far end of town.

15

Another one of those days. I woke at 4 in the morning, the sheets pooled at my feet. I reached for the glass of water, my throat prickly as a cactus. I laid in bed and stared at the ceiling, counting bumps in the texture. I had dreamed—maybe nightmared—and shreds of it still clung to the back of my mind.

"Bad dream?"

I turned toward the sound of the voice, the smells of roses and myrrh.

"What do you want, Gabriel?"

I heard her shrug in the dark. I had to play this cool if I wanted to know where Cory was. She was skittish on the best days, and with the scars between us, any hint I'd been looking for her, she'd bolt. Best to pretend she was an annoyance instead of an asset.

"What do I always want?" She asked.

"Me?"

"Think highly of yourself, don't you?"

"You used to."

She smiled in the dark, her teeth gleaming in the ambient light. I loved her smile. I wasn't sure how I felt about her anymore. Abandonment will do that, color your opinion of a person, poison that well.

She sighed, and the smell of myrrh strengthened. "I heard about your problems. Does this mean you're back?"

"Jesus." I rolled on my back. "Do you have eyes everywhere? On second thought—don't answer that. Look, just tell me where I can find Cory."

She continued like she hadn't heard me. "How many more beatings can you take, Jack? How long before you slip? Before you forget a rune, mispronounce a Word?"

"And you want me to retire? Settle down with a nice...whatever it is you are, is that it? Where were you before this, then? Shouldn't you have been offering me cake and wine instead of a broke-ass life on the south side?"

She sighed again. She was getting irritated. There was a rustle, and the room was empty. I wondered about the intelligence of pissing off a Divine and decided I didn't care. I cursed, realizing she hadn't answered my question. I wondered how long before the café down the street was open and settled myself for a long day.

———

The café opened at six. I made it down by six-thirty. I found a table in the back corner, poorly lit, cigarette burns on the linoleum top, a light film on the finish I didn't want to know about.

The waitress came by, tired eyes and attitude. "What do you want?"

"Coffee. Black."

"Breakfast?"

I looked at her. She was staring sullenly at me over the pad. I wanted to say something about how I would be glad to order the special of the day if I didn't have to kill it, talk to her again, or suppress the urge to poke her in the eyes. Instead, I just shook my head, and she slouched off. I made a note to check the coffee for floaters and waited.

The coffee came, the waitress's mood noticeably improved. She even smiled when I said thank you, her lips turning up, her nose crinkling. I could see the coke in her nostrils, and just sat back, sipping the coffee. It wasn't bad.

Half an hour and two cups later, the bells on the door clanged, and the old priest came in. Demonites have churches, just like everyone else. If you were to walk into one, the trappings would even look familiar. But after a while, you'll notice things that don't belong. The baptismal in the wrong spot. Votives the wrong color. Service never seems to be held. And the plaster Jesus that adorns so many places of worship would strike you as wrong somehow. Maybe a little madness in the eyes, a little rage in the set of the mouth. Demonites are a lot of things, but we believe in the truth. And the truth of a god being tortured to death, then eating the sin of the world isn't pretty.

The other big difference—they keep guys like me on the payroll to clean up messes caused by members of the Umbra. Especially the Vessels—men and women susceptible to possession or incredible feats. Things you might call miracles, and the rest of us call a huge pain in the ass. Think of a demonite church like a supernatural CIA branch, and you get the idea. I'd left that life behind a long time ago. But you can never really escape from your past.

The priest found me right away, something that never ceased to amaze me. A charity had offered him a seeing-eye dog some time back. He had refused, saying if the Lord wanted him to see, he would've given him eyes instead of a massive dick. One of his favorites, if I recall right. Absolutely horrified the Karens on the church committee.

He sat, his hands finding the cup I had bought for him. Two sugars, creamer. He took a sip and grimaced.

"This tastes like shit, Jack."

"Does being blind affect your taste buds, too?"

He smiled, and let it slip after a time. "I never see you anymore. Are you back, then?"

I stared down at the cup in my hands, let the obvious joke go. "I'm not welcome, anymore. You know that, Bill."

"Have you ever tried to make amends? Come halfway?"

"I know you didn't come all this way just to lecture me. What is it?"

"Gabriel."

"What about her? She stops in to annoy me, remind me I'm old, washed up. Remind me I'm not welcome, then disappears."

Bill grimaced. He did that sometimes, especially when he heard something distasteful. "I wish you wouldn't do that."

"Do what?"

"Quantify things. Nothing's black and white. Haven't you learned anything?"

"Okay, so maybe you did come here to lecture me. So you're saying the Vessels aren't black and white?"

"I'm just saying things aren't always what you make them out to be."

He stood and made his way back to the door. Halfway there, he turned around, and focused his cataracts dead on me.

"I love you, Jack. Now stop being an ass."

The bell chimed, and he was gone. I took a sip of coffee, but it had gone cold.

16

The alley smelled of wine and garbage. An open grate spilled steam into the street. I picked my way among the refuse and rats, trying not to smash the cardboard boxes or disturb the men huddled in twos and threes or under layers of newspaper.

I glanced up at the sky self-consciously and turned the corner, a slight unease settling in the pit of my stomach. I wasn't supposed to be here. And not because I wasn't exactly homeless, but because of who ran this part of town.

Another 30 yards of despair, and I saw him. The Prophet, Man of Sorrows. Down on his luck and looking none the worse for wear. He smiled through a scraggle of long dirty hair, and his teeth shone white.

"Jack," he said.

As if he'd been expecting me the whole time. He probably had.

He patted a filthy pile of newspaper next to him, bidding me take a seat. I hunkered down, and he passed a bottle of indeterminate origin to me. I shook it a bit, held it up to the light.

"Still with the wine?" I asked him.

"Nectar of the gods."

I handed it back to him.

"Still with the not drinking?"

"I'm on the clock."

I felt the weight of the Sig bumping against my ribs. He looked at me and shook his head, then reached out and tapped the gun through my jacket.

"Nasty habit you got there," he said.

"You too. I thought you were out of the judgement business."

"You didn't come here to bicker."

I sighed. "No. I met Bill today. He came to say something about Gabriel, but I chased him off. Changed the subject."

"You burn your bridges nicely." Silence for a minute. Then, "Does this mean you're back?"

I shook my head. "Everyone keeps asking me. No. I just need to find someone. Then I'm out again."

He held up his hands, the bandages covering his palms made of torn strips of t-shirt. They were filthy, brown and black in places, the dirt dried and flaking, yet still red and moist in the centers. On the left one I could make out the word "Jive," folded and twisted somewhat.

"Sacrifice." He said, his eyes holding mine.

Something in the alley rustled. His eyes snapped from mine to the space behind me.

"Run."

I didn't ask why, knew if I did there would be no more questions. Ever. I bolted into the dark behind his seat, loosing the Sig from its mooring, feeling the weight in my hand like a coiled serpent. I flicked the safety off and wondered if even the runes would hold the fucker I knew was coming.

Boxes and bodies flashed by me, dirty brick to my left and right, a brown sky overhead, brown mud beneath. I heard my breath after the first few yards, and the sucking sound of mud being displaced. I spun right, into an alcove, and brought the Sig to eye level. Something blew past, impossibly fast, raising the puddles in the alley into a v-shaped wake, the wind ruffling my hair. Then, silence, but for heartbeat and breath.

I lowered the pistol and sighted down the center of the alley. Slow breath, in, then out, long and easy. My finger tightened on the trigger, and I squeezed. The report echoed like thunder in the confines, and then the smells of cordite, and blood, and a ringing in my ears filled my senses.

I felt the wind shift when it turned, saw the hole I had made. Then the red wound became a blur, and the thing was coming for me, the mud and debris blowing behind it like a gale.

"Shit." I'd just pissed it off.

The bricks to my left exploded in an orange powder, and I dropped, rolling to my right. A bit too slow. I felt a new gash in my shoulder where the thing had sliced me. It throbbed once, and I gasped, my vision blurring.

I crouched in the mud, the Sig still wisping smoke in the cool air, my breath following suit. I felt the blood trickle from my shoulder, and saw a puddle turning a deep red from the corner of my eye.

The alley was quiet. I hated this. Goddamn Vessel. The circle on my back itched, and I tucked and rolled, tasting snow and dirt. The space I had occupied a moment before shattered into frag-ments of slush and concrete, the Vessel hammering the ground with such force I felt the vibration in the soles of my shoes.

I snapped the Sig up and sprayed the alley left to right, brick turning to powder and craters where the rounds struck, the shells sizzling and turning the water where they fell to steam.

I rolled again, and felt the wind snap past me, its breath on my neck. I crouched for a moment, shivering in the cool air. I was soaked, cold, and pissed, and getting nowhere fast. Uttering a short prayer to anyone listening, I lowered the Sig's barrel into the mud and spun, cutting a crude circle into the ground.

Almost...

Down the alley, I saw the water rising, the Vessel gaining

speed. That's why it hadn't attacked yet. Sadistic fuck wanted to play with me first.

I reached inside my jacket and stuck my fingers into the wound. My vision blurred again, and I nearly passed out, head swimming like I'd been hit with a sledge.

Almost...

It was closer, the wound in its abdomen dripping red, streaming down what appeared to be a bird's leg, the details blurred by speed and the haze in my sight.

I dripped the blood on my fingers into the groove I had made in the snow and spoke the Word. The circle enflamed, a cylinder of blazing blue fire setting the alley alight and scorching my retinas for half a minute. Okay by me. I didn't have to see to know what was coming next.

The Vessel slammed into the barrier full force, and shattered, the flames scorching its flesh to cinders even before its scream had stopped echoing off the close walls. I broke the circle, and the flames extinguished, leaving the alley dark and dank again, a smell like burnt horse hooves in the air.

I staggered over to the wall and slid down, sitting full in the mud. My shoulder hurt like hell, my ass was soaking wet, and I felt like nodding out. Well, one out of three ain't bad. I closed my eyes and slept.

17

I napped in the alley for two hours. When your body says 'stop,' and you don't, it hits the brakes regardless. I guessed the Prophet and his men had kept watch. Nice policy of non-interdiction, that.

"Oh sure, we'll let you fight the big scary monster with razor-sharp talons and big pointy teeth, then watch you take a nap. You're welcome."

I staggered to my feet and wandered back to the hotel. The desk clerk ignored me, as was policy in a place like this, and I made my way down the hall. I opened the door to my room, and stepped in. The envelope was the same as all the others, plain manila with a wax seal. I picked it up from the floor. They always seemed to know when I was out, when to slide the message in. I considered it a bit of an insult they never deigned to speak to me. I considered it even more of an insult they'd think I was back.

I dropped the envelope on the table, and sat across from it, gathering my thoughts. I hadn't seen one of these in years, since the church and I had been quit. Whatever it was had to be serious business for them to call on me in the middle of all this. I took another look at the envelope.

The wax was red, the symbol inscribed on it arcane. I never completely understood the security. Anyone who broke into the apartment would not be looking for an envelope. Even if they did take it, they wouldn't know what to do with the contents. Still, better safe than sorry and all that shit.

I looked at the tattoo on my palm, the one matching the symbol. I concentrated until it was in my mind's eye, blazing like a sun, then pressed my hand against the seal. There was a flare, and the wax melted, ran, and evaporated. The flap separated from the paper with an audible pop.

My hand was still smoking, so I dipped it under the faucet, listening to the sizzle die. When the last wisps had disappeared, I returned to the table and picked up the envelope, weighing the contents.

I hated this part. This was the part where I found out who I had to kill. Vessel by nature, do not know they are such. They don't go around committing extreme good or extreme evil on purpose—it just happens for them. It would be different if they were the personification of their alignment, but for most—hell, almost all—they were like anyone else.

They had jobs, wives, kids, bills, and worries. The problem was each was a tip of the scales. They were the people you would see standing at disasters—plane crashes, fires, homicides, rapes—you name it. You could count on them being there because something in their nature pulled them to the site. They were the reason tragedy and miracles happened—for every fire, a baby lives; for every homicide, a victim survives.

But they tipped the scales, and in doing so, upset the balance.

The other problem with a Vessel is they would inspire others to extremes without knowing why. A Vessel might complain about a poorly cooked burger and spawn a serial killer. Another may praise the worker and create a man who relieves famine.

Then there were their deaths. Some Vessel attracted beings who didn't belong on this plane. They would wait, until the moment of death, devouring the Vessel's soul as it escaped, growing fat on power. They would then reanimate the body and attempt to go about life, hoping for a second chance. At what, I've never been sure. Always, always, always, this turned out to be a pain in the ass for yours truly.

I opened the packet and shook out the contents. Two rune rounds. A photo. I turned it over, my stomach turning when I saw the face, the eyes. Something was blurring my vision, and I felt a tear roll down my cheek.

I turned the photo over, my hands shaking again. I told myself it was age. I was getting too old. This is just another Vessel, I told myself. Just another body. Just another…

The thought trailed off. Bullshit. I was already Exile. If I didn't do it, what could they do? Exile me again?

"There are things in Heaven and Hell not dreamt of in your philosophy, Jack. I hear they reserve them for the ones who defy twice."

Gabriel.

I kept my back to her, rubbing my eyes, trying to appear tired.

"Stay out of my head. I hate it when you do that."

She took the chair across from me.

"I'm sorry," she apologized. "It's hard when your emotions float your thoughts like that."

She picked up the shells, rolling them in her palm.

"It's amazing how much more damage words and feelings can do the heart than these little things."

She let them fall to the table, each hitting and ringing in a single clear note.

"Has two millennia made you that crass?" I asked her.

"Has being on the outside made you weak, Jack?"

"Maybe it has. Maybe I still remember what love is. Maybe I've tired of living with one hand dipped in blood."

She changed the subject. "Heard you had a run-in today."

"Who sent it, Gabriel? Was it Cory? Where is he?"

She shrugged.

"Bullshit. You knew about it. How?"

"The Prophet told me. To his credit, he was reluctant to share. He's very protective of you, Jack."

A long pause.

"Why him?" It was my turn to change the subject, and I dropped a finger on the photo.

She looked. Shrugged. I wondered if her shoulders were tired of her lack of commitment yet.

"He's a Vessel. Isn't that enough? You knew better than to make friends, Jack. You knew from the day you took the tattoos. The day you agreed to the task, you knew the job at hand," she said.

"I do this, and what? I get Cory?"

"You do this, it's a step in the right direction," she said.

"Fuck. You."

I said it without looking at her, and I knew it would piss her off. I didn't have to turn my head to know she was gone.

Two in the afternoon, and I was tired. Too damn tired. This was taking too long. Whatever Cory was up to had to be gaining steam while I played keep away with Gabriel.

I started to wish for a good single malt, a quiet night, and a soft bed. I picked up one of the shells, rolling it in my palm, around and around. After a time, I loaded it, and its companion, tore some clean bedding for a bandage, and left again. I had a job to do, after all.

18

It took me nearly four hours to find my way back to the Prophet's alley. I took a few back routes to be safe. I paused at the entrance, the falling dark doing little to mask the scents and the feel wafting from the confines. The Sig found its way into my palm, the Pachmayr grips digging in. I popped the safety and stepped in.

It was quieter than normal, even with the men on pallets snoring, and the soft rustle of paper in a night breeze. The alley felt warmer, and the mud beneath my feet loose. I stepped further in and took a breath. Every time, it was hard to see him. He had forgiven, maybe not forgotten, and though he had changed his name, (this time it was John Christmas), it was always hard to look into his eyes.

I turned the corner and saw it. A crucifix of pipe and wire in an X, the Man of Sorrows living up to his name. Small pipes had been inserted into his veins, and he bled to the ground, the flow little more than a trickle, the blood heating the alley.

I felt the Sig slip from my hand, and I dropped to my knees. He lifted his head and looked, pupils blind. When his lips opened, the sound was little more than a whisper, but I heard every word.

"Therefore, behold days are coming, says the Lord, when this place will no longer be called Topheth or Ben-Hinnom Valley, but the Valley of Slaughter."

My hand found the Sig, and I did what had to be done.

I killed him again.

I wept in the alley, the light of the moon mingling with the river of blood, shades of red illuminating the world. In time, I staggered free from the confines, and leaned against the wall. The Prophet's blood clung to my hands, and I wiped them in slow half circles on each side of the alley. I knew what I was doing and did not care. When it was complete, the sigil looked like a red circle cut by blackness.

"Tabach."

The word slipped from my lips like the echo of a thunderstorm, the circle glowing and smoking until the brick turned white.

"Chathah."

The white became a sun, and the blaze exploded down the alley, a river of argent fire. There were no screams, no time to wake and run, and nowhere to run. It was quick, cleansing, and utterly complete. You can argue the men there were innocent, blameless in this. But to stand aside and let this tragedy happen— God may forgive, but I couldn't. Not then.

I knew I'd have to pay penance someday for the person I'd become, but until then, I was happy to rack up the debt.

———

St. Anthony's. Patron of the lost. The irony wasn't wasted.

The church was cold and dark, the pews lined before the altar like worshippers on Sunday. Hymnals and dark wood, hard floors and vaulted ceiling, the whole thing gave me the creeps, the idea man could and would try to contain God in a structure, in an idea.

Behind the altar, white and shining softly in colored moon-light let in by stained glass set high in the wall, a pool of crystal water rippled in murmurs against its tile prison.

I stepped to the edge of the baptismal and saw the trail, burgundy in the light, drops spreading like slow mist, turning consecrated water to wine. It flowed steadily from the tiled edge of the water to steps leading from the dais to a small door in the wall.

I heard rustling, and felt the Sig in my grip before I was aware I had slipped it free. I stepped to the door, hands sweating, the grips growing slick, but clinging, nonetheless.

One breath; two.

The doorknob was in my hand, and I twisted, the metal slipping a bit, the tongue making louder a noise than I would've liked. The door swung open, and I stopped.

Gabriel.

She perched on the chair behind Bill, her lips and chin red with his life, his sockets empty, eyes torn free, the orbitals chewed, his chest a ragged hole. She held the remains of his heart in her hand, talons piercing the tender flesh.

I lifted the pistol, the trigger nearly squeezing itself, shattering the chair, hammering the wood into splinters.

She was fast, maybe faster than me, and she shifted to the side, then forward, her body moving in a blur, talons raking my chest. I threw myself sideways and pounded the air with lead again. Then she was there, on top of me, the long, forked tongue licking at my face, probing my eyes.

I shoved, and she flew backwards. I brought the pistol up again. It kicked once, and she squealed, a hurt animal sound. Then, breaking glass, and wings. Silence settled in, and I slumped to the floor.

I listened to the wind sigh through the window. After a time, I looked at Bill, his gaze blank and empty. I couldn't leave him there to be filled with whatever came across the veil.

"Same shit, different day, old buddy."
I shot the corpse in the head and left.
Better safe than sorry, and all that shit.

19

B ack at the hotel, the room was dark and empty. I hadn't expected her to return. I gathered the few things I needed into a pack and burned the rest. Outside, the wind had begun to pick up, and rain blew in waves across the pavement.

I found an empty warehouse across town, the inside dank and cool, rusted steel and aluminum its only inhabitants. I cut a circle into the floor and shifted space, coming out in the same warehouse, slightly rustier, metal pockmarked by wind and age, sand dusting the floor.

Outside, it was noon, the sun bright and hot, the sands rolling in every direction equally so. In the distance, I saw the station's silhouette, and moved that way, the silt slipping beneath my feet, the wind covering my tracks. This was the In-Between. It was neutral ground for Heaven and Hell, and the denizens and outcasts of both came here to escape the grind.

After an hour, sand gave way to cobblestone, and cobblestone to a wood platform, grey with age and weather. Behind it, a ramshackle shed with a glass window. Behind the window sat an old man, his skin grey as the wood, his head bald with tufts of white hair. He looked up, wire-rimmed glasses perched on the end of his nose, the green visor on his head throwing his face into a Christmas hue.

"Eh?" He asked.

"One for the Shards."

"Round-trip?"

"One way."

I pushed a few coins across the counter, hexagonal, and made of a metal that hadn't been discovered yet. He took them, bit into one, and pushed a button. The machine under the counter coughed, and spit out a ticket, pale blue, printed with the icon of grasses. I took it and found a bench on the platform.

I waited, staring out at the sands, and thinking of nothing. After a time, I felt the chair beneath me vibrate, and I readied my pack. In the distance I saw what looked like a heat mirage, the air shimmering and shaking. A sound followed it, a sort of *whump whump* growing louder by the second.

As I watched, the air split from the center of the mirage outward, a hole behind which I could see only darkness. From it, the *whump* had turned into a *CHUG*, and I saw a light burning in the dark, approaching at speed.

There was a sound like thunder, and the air split fully, black blotting the sun for an instant as the veil parted, the light from the train a sun in itself. Then another deep boom, and the train was there, steaming and hissing on the tracks, the black gone, the landscape once again desert.

From the car in front of me a door opened, and a tall man, dressed in a black frock and wearing a flat-brim hat, stepped down. I stood, and he stretched a hand out, skeletal fingers opening on a palm of parchment flesh. I retrieved a coin from my pocket, round and gold, its surface smooth as the sky. His fingers closed, and he stepped to the side, allowing me to board the train.

Inside, the train was dark and cool, red velvet seats and dim lights. The paneling was black, the floorboards a cool lacquered oak. I made my way past the other passengers, most the souls of men and women who had passed recently, though here and there others, Divine and otherwise, had joined the journey for reasons of their own.

I passed a tall, pale creature, his features little more than slits in a white face, on pilgrimage from the Sea, the gills in his neck flickering occasionally; a couple dressed in clothes from the 20's, and a wraith, ghostly flesh peeling from ghostly bones, his eyes and mouth seeping grey smoke. At the back of the car was a lone bench, and I sat down, pack in my lap, and waited.

The train pulled out, sand and sun rolling, and then flashing by, blending to orange and yellow. There was a flash, and a rolling boom, and the landscape turned dark. We were in the cairn-noir, the landscape nothing more than shadows built on shadows. I laid back, knowing my stop was the last on the line, and closed my eyes.

20

The car rocked gently on phantom tracks. The clink of glasses and ice, poker chips and speech, and the steady breathing of sleeping passengers lulled me into rest. I dreamed of things long dead, of Gabriel and Gideon, the twins, and of the Sea where we all had been born. I dreamed of the light and days before the light, and finally, we were at the Shards, and I woke.

I stepped off the train, the town stretching before the platform built in the style of adobe homes, all the color of brick. Even the ground here, hard-packed clay, was a reddish-orange that absorbed the light above and held it, until the path seemed to glow. I pulled my pack over my shoulder and stepped into town, red dust clinging to my shoes and jeans almost as soon as I stepped foot in.

At the entrance to town were a line of merchant's stands, wood, with a white cloth awning over each. Some had lined their wares up on makeshift counters, some hung them from poles supporting the awnings, each seeming to vie for strangeness over the others.

At the end of the street, something big moved into the shadows of a building, and I followed, digging in my pack for the

Sig. A quick right turn, and I was in the alley, pistol out and ready. *He* was there, tucked into a corner—well, as much as four hundred pounds of muscle can tuck, staring at me.

"Jack."

He looked rough, his skin black from the sun, cracked like the desert floor. From between the cracks, blue light shone weakly, smoke wafting occasionally from a fissure. He spoke again, glowing eyes and mouth ebbing and peaking like a tide.

"It's been too long," he said.

"Gideon. You look… well, I don't want to use the phrase 'like hammered shit,' but here we are."

He chuckled, low and liquid, like water over gravel.

"You look like shit, too, friend."

He shifted positions, the plates on his skin making sounds like stone on steel. He came to rest cross-legged on the ground. I slipped the Sig back into my pack and approached. After what seemed like a moment of consideration, he placed his palms on the ground, and spoke a Word. The earth lifted itself up in a small wave, contouring and shifting until it formed a chair. He smiled.

"Sit."

I sat, and felt the earth shift itself under me until it felt like a gentle palm was cradling me.

"You've learned a few new things since last we met."

He shook his head. "No. Just things I had forgotten."

I sighed. "Speaking of…"

"How is my sister?" he interrupted.

"So, you haven't forgotten. She's…unwell."

He looked away, toward the sky. Without looking back, he replied.

"I feared as much. It was Samael, wasn't it?"

I felt a knot of ice in the pit of my stomach. I hadn't considered the Blind God. Had I fucked up that deeply? Something—instinct maybe—shrugged. Did it matter? Could I have stopped it?

Shut up, I thought, resenting the idea my free will was an illusion.

I turned back to Gideon. He was studying me, as if trying to read my thoughts.

"What happened?" he asked.

"Your sister overstepped her bounds. She killed a Vessel out of turn and attacked me. Gideon, you should know—she's feral. I caught her eating the Vessel's viscera."

He turned away, the flames in his eyes dimming to as near dark as possible. I thought about interrupting, thought better than to disturb the Divine in his grief. After a time, he turned back, his eyes glowing again, the fire somehow deeper, more intense.

"Find Nial. He'll know what to do. He's in the Shards to the west of here—the basalt forest, I believe."

I stood and turned to go.

"Jack. When you find the—the thing, behind this, you make it hurt."

"And your sister?"

He was quiet. I knew the answer.

———

The basalt forest was a maze of black pillars dividing the end of the wastes and the Weeping Sands from the lava fields and obsidian archipelagos comprising the Shards. I made my way there, wrapping a scarf around my face to keep the blowing sands from my lungs as I walked.

Occasionally, I would pass a body, preserved by the sands, still looking fresh as the day it died. I made wide berths around these, knowing especially in the land of the dead, the dead didn't stay that way.

The first of the pillars rose before me, blotting the sun. The black spire was backlit by a corona of fire. It left pinpricks of light in my vision when I looked away, and I wondered for a minute why the hell I'd looked at it in the first place.

In the forest, even the wind seemed to die, and the shadows cast by the pillars cooled the air. I dropped the scarf from my face. The air tasted of seawater. The atmosphere was electric, making my skin prickle in gooseflesh, the hair on the back of my neck rise. This was a sacred place, one of power, and I felt it beating in the rock around me.

I meandered toward the center of the forest, the rock growing stranger and more twisted as I did so, runes—some I recognized, some I didn't—appearing with greater frequency, carved into the stone by tools alien to Earth.

As I walked, the thrum I felt earlier became a full-fledged beat. The rhythm pulsed in the air, its power a tangible thing, running like blood through the passages forming the veins of the forest. The pillars began to clear, more cohesive in formation, the spacing regular and wider, opening into a clearing of little more than a few yards across.

I halted there aware the Sig would do me no good. I scanned the area, my eyes settling on a figure dwarfed by the stone. He sat cross-legged on the ground, a cowled robe hiding his features. I started across the clearing, and made it halfway when a voice, soft, yet clear as a bell, sounded in the air around me.

"Gideon sent you."

Not a question. I felt the power in the place, tense, coiled. He was wary. I worried a bit, knowing what he was capable of. I wondered if the disease had begun to shake him.

"Yes." I said.

"The girl. She is with the one you know as Ramirez."

"Are you sure?" I knew he wasn't lying. Part of me just didn't want to confirm it.

There was a low rumble from Nial's end of the valley. I held up my hands.

"Okay, okay."

Nial spoke again. "One thing. A favor if you will."

"Gideon never mention—"

"One thing is not too much to ask, is it, Exile?"

I sighed. I still remembered the last time someone asked me to do one thing. Turned out to be a doozy of a favor.

"When you finish the Divine, put her down permanently."

"And Ramirez?"

"What is it to you, Exile? Are you not kindred spirits?"

"Kindred like you and leprosy."

Thunder again, louder this time. The air seemed ready to snap.

"Get out."

The words came like the breaking of a storm, heavy and laden with electricity, forming a palpable weight in the air. There was a feeling of pressure, like a mountain had been set on my chest, and the next second, I found myself back at the station.

"Well," I said to no one in particular. "That's handy."

21

I left the way I came, through the old warehouse, cutting the circle into the concrete with a nail from one of the long-rotted timbers.

I came out in the middle of a mountain range, blues and whites tinting earth and sky—the wind blowing snow in drifts falling over the cliffs in long-fingered plumes. In the distance, a building, long and low to the ground and surrounded by hurricane fence, squatted on the mountainside like a low cloud.

Ramirez was here.

I wasn't sure how I knew—maybe it was something Nial had planted there, maybe it was instinct. Still, he was here.

I started across the snowscape, staggering into the wind until I could feel no more than my eyes and nose stinging in the cold, my vision turning white. I flexed my fingers and wished for a scarf and wondered how they would find my body.

Then I was there, cold steel clenched in already painful hands, the chain-links surrounding the prison seeming to clutch back. I cleared the ice from my eyebrows and nose and looked up. Towers stood at the four corners of the enclosed yard, and a gate, set into the fence, stood quiet and unoccupied. I found it odd no one manned the outside, despite the weather. This was a prison, after all.

I pushed on the gate, and it swung open, making a groove in the snow where the bottom links hung. In the near distance, the building seemed squatter than it had, as though it had gained a personal gravity drawing in everything surrounding it and then shat it out in a world built in a funhouse mirror. Even the few sparse trees clinging to the yard were twisted out of true, trunks and limbs reaching for no sky in particular, the bark curled as though only half-peeled.

The effect made me queasy—and a bit dizzy. I closed my eyes and let the world spin behind my lids. The bag slid from my shoulder, and I rummaged around, feeling about for the Sig. It only took a moment, and the pistol was there, the grips digging into my flesh. It helped to steady me, and the nausea slowed from a roil to a bubbling. I took a deep breath and readied myself to look at the world again.

From what I guessed was the entrance to the prison came the sound of footsteps in the snow, and the quiet jangle of chains. I opened my eyes, pistol swinging up. It took a minute to adjust to what I was seeing.

Two figures. A man, about six feet and stocky, held a chain leash. I followed the links down, and the pistol dipped, my hand shaking more than I normally would have been happy with.

It was Gabriel, her white hair disheveled, and matted in places by mud and blood. Her eyes bulged with madness, and her tongue, long and forked, lolled from her mouth, lips frozen in a rictus grin. She sat on her haunches like a dog, her hands buried in the snow. Already I saw the scales growing up the sides of her face—a sign her feral nature was taking a firm hold. She didn't seem to mind.

Ramirez gestured.

"Sorry about your friend here, but when I found her, she was half-frozen, and almost dead. Seems those bullets of yours can be anathema to one of her... nature. So, I took her in, fed her. She's a very good girl."

He reached down and ruffled her hair.

Why can't I shoot?

There was a click, and the leash dropped free. She leapt, claws extended, wings snapping open and blowing the snow in twin whirlwinds behind her.

Like that, I was free of my paralysis, and I spun to the side, the pistol coming up. Something still kept me from firing, and I reversed the weapon, bringing it down in a blow that would've crushed a man's skull. I felt it connect, and she squealed and veered in the air, slamming into the ground not far away.

I saw the opening and leapt, Regnos lending me strength. I landed with my knees in her back, my hands on the pinions closest to her shoulders.

"I'm sorry," I said.

I tore upward, the muscles in my arms burning, the tattoos lending me strength blazing until they had burnt holes even through my clothes. At first, there was resistance, and then they came, the wings separating from muscle, blood staining already dirty feathers red, my hands looking as though they had been bathed in ochre.

She screamed, high and keening, a sound that could have shattered glass and eardrum alike, and I clutched at my head, losing my balance as she rolled, pinning me beneath her. Her claws tore at my eyes, and I raised my arms to shield myself, the wards there flaring and singeing her flesh until the air was filled only with screams and the stench of cooked Divine.

I kicked upward, knocking her far back enough to scramble away. Then she was up again and tearing at me with the speed of a Vessel. I grabbed the Sig from where it lay in the snow, my body doing the rest. As she neared, I twisted, the barrel plugging her screaming mouth, stopping her dead. She looked at me, shocked, and for a moment, I thought I saw the old Gabriel. Something stung my eyes.

Then I pulled the trigger.

Crimson and white, and her body fell in slow motion, landing in the snow like a leaf fallen from a tree. I couldn't see any more, and I felt the strength in my limbs giving out. I chanted a Word, and tore the Veil between worlds, dropping onto a rain-slick street. I used the last of my strength to dig out the phone and tap a message to Ivy, then let it fall to the asphalt.

In the distance, sirens.

22

I woke in a hospital bed, Ivy beside me. She gave me a glare that could have wilted the Hulk's tackle. I grinned sheepishly.

"You get your ass kicked a lot, you know that?" She asked. "But every time, you come back with just a little more of the puzzle."

She tossed a slip of paper on my sheet. I picked it up. A name was written in Gabrielle's hand. Escher's Rest. I didn't know why she would've written it. Maybe it was a warning. Maybe it was a clue, left in her last moments of lucidity. I did know for an aching second, I felt the loss like a knife. Then I walled that part off. Gabriel had been lost long before I showed up.

"How'd I get here?" I asked.

"I brought you, as usual."

I looked at the IV in my hand, the wires running from my chest. I raised my hand and gestured with it.

"At least I know why I feel floaty."

"Good, then you won't be pissed when I tell you this: ask for help. You're going to get yourself killed, and I'm a good witch, but I'm not that good. The only thing you're useful for after that is reagents."

"I'm wounded. You would use my kidney for evil?"

"I would use your kidney for profit."

"Horse apiece. But I get your point."

She reached out and took my hand, squeezed it. Her fingers were warm, soft. We sat in silence until the drugs took me under again.

———

The nurse woke me by pulling the IV from my arm. I ached again, but not as much. Narcotics. Who knew? I mean, aside from everyone that's ever taken them. For once though, they'd left my dreams alone, and I was grateful.

"Hey, I was using that," I said.

He smiled, tight-lipped. "Time to go, Mr. Nyx. Here are your discharge instructions," he shoved a pile of papers into my hand, "and your clothes are in the closet. The doctor's given you a prescription for pain. Make a follow-up with your provider in two weeks."

Nurse Ratched disappeared, and I got dressed, getting my things together. Nothing like American healthcare. I expected a bill the size of one of those fantasy novels Ivy liked so much to arrive tomorrow. I slipped from the room and out the front door. Ivy was just pulling the car around, and I sank into it gratefully.

"Where to?" She asked.

"Escher's Rest. Ramirez is alive."

"What?"

I nodded. "I knew something didn't feel right, and now I know what it is. The old man and Cory have been playing us."

We stopped by her apartment to pick up a couple of things. Ivy had a go-bag, and I needed clothing that fit, a thing she fixed by rolling her eyes and tossing a handful of dust at me in the parking garage. Whatever she'd done to the suit caused it to adjust itself on my body, a sensation making me cringe internally as even the boxers tailored themselves. When it finished, I made her make a detour.

The stop was to a fence I'd met in the joint. Tank was a short black man with more acne scars than Sears has lawnmowers. Trust me, that joke kills in the Midwest. Ivy stayed in the car—I'd convinced her Tank was jumpy. Which was only partially true. He liked to reminisce about prison, and I'd prefer to keep that bit to myself.

He greeted me with a nod, legs hanging off the oversize bumper of his slate-gray van. He gave me a grin, teeth white in his broad olive face.

"If it ain't Nugs."

Fuck, I'd nearly forgotten about that. I'd hoped he had.

"Hey man, you remember why we called you Nugs?"

"Smuggled a whole ten-piece in a pair of pants. Yeah, I remember. How you doin', Tank?"

"Good, man. You need me to hook you up?"

He hopped from the bumper and cracked the doors. Shelves and pockets had been built into the sides of the van, and they held all manner of items, from military-grade weaponry to blades to blenders. I looked them over for a minute, frowned when I didn't see what I needed.

"What you need, man?" Tank asked.

"Blackball," I said.

Tank whistled, looked thoughtful. A blackball was pretty much what it sounded like. A sphere about the size of an eight-ball, cut and polished from obsidian. It could be used to trap a spirit or force a cleansing.

"Don't get much call for those. You got the cash?"

"I'll have to owe you."

He appeared to consider it. I'd known Tank a long time and knew two things about the man. He liked cash. Harder to trace, easy to spend. And the only thing he liked more than cash were favors from useful people. Finally, he nodded, and ran his hand over the floor of the van. There was a soft *click*, and a panel popped open. He reached inside, pulling a couple of objects out: a finger with an oversized ring trapped between swollen knuckles, a tiny skull with sharp canines, and finally, the blackball.

He passed it over to me, and I held it for a minute. It was heavy and cold, the depths endless despite the mirror shine. Just holding it in my hand, I felt a gentle tug from the sphere, as if it would be so easy for my spirit to slip from my skin and rest there.

I wrapped it in a handkerchief and stowed it in my inside suit pocket. I held out a hand, and Tank took it.

"Deal," he said. "Your number the same?"

I shook my head. "Place burned down. I'll get in touch as soon as I have a cell."

He nodded. "Good enough. Don't wait too long. I can always find work for a guy like you."

"Fair enough," I said.

We made our goodbyes, then I hopped into Ivy's Beamer.

"Get it?" She asked.

I nodded, and we rolled from the alley and into traffic. The radio was playing something by Marvin Gaye. We rode in silence for a while, Otis and Fogerty keeping us company. The city passed by in decreasing density, trees replacing the buildings, fields and lawns sidewalks and parking lots. Escher's Rest was a two-day drive from town, and we had a lot of highway to cover.

———

"That suit trick," I said, breaking the silence.

"Comes in handy," she said.

I narrowed my eyes. "How handy?"

"If you're implying I keep those clothes around because I have sex with a lot of men, you're treading on dangerous ground. I wasn't a nun before you stumbled your gangly cracker ass into my life."

I suddenly felt like a man who's discovered his pants are full of bees and decided not to slap myself in the groin.

"So uh," I said, changing the subject with all the tact of a flaming rhinoceros, "Aren't you worried about your apartment?"

She looked over for a minute, one eyebrow cocked. I felt the weight of an asskicking there. Finally, she quirked a smile.

"The wards on that place would incinerate the first idiot who tried," she said. "Granted, if they managed to crack them, I have renter's insurance, too. You know, like a normal person."

"Ivy, my room was above a cut-rate butcher's. The cockroaches were too busy fighting the rats over who got the leftovers. My unofficial roommate was a guy who called himself Captain Superstar and slept in the hall and sometimes left me boxes of his hair. The only thing insurance would cover is the cost of the landlord disposing of my charred corpse."

"That's a shame."

"We all have our crosses to bear. Mine was the smell of burning hair."

She snorted a laugh, and the miles rolled by.

———

Night fell, and we needed to stop for food and rest. There was a greasy diner at the halfway point, and we treated ourselves to burgers—the real kind, hand-shaped and topped with thick slices of cheddar—and milkshakes, thick and rich. Islands of calm. That's what my mother called them. Islands of calm in a storm. All around you the wind blows, the rain hammers down, but here—here it's just good food and serenity.

A little further down the road, we found a motel shaped like a U. The paint and trim were peeling, the windows dirty. Still, cars and trucks occupied nearly every space before the doors in the lot. Ivy went in and got us the room, as I didn't have a credit card. Because A) My credit's not what you'd call stellar, and B) I didn't like anything that let the government know when you bought a taco, towels, or took a shit.

When she came out, her expression was carefully guarded.

"Just the one room," she said.

I sighed in relief. "Thought you were gonna tell me I had to sleep with the clerk."

She led us to a door with the paint scratched off in a variety of interesting and obscene ways. She unlocked it with a real key, as opposed to a mag-lock card.

"I didn't think they even made those things anymore," I said. "Did we travel back in time? Is this 1955?"

"Fuck that noise," she said.

I looked at her, blinked. Black woman in the 50s. "Ah, yeah, because of the McCarthyism," I said.

She let a sardonic laugh and let us in. The interior of the room was somewhat better than the exterior, though the décor probably hadn't been updated since the 70s. Everything was shag, and what wasn't shag was an odd color of yellow. The air was stale, but the tub and the single bed were clean.

"One bed, huh?" I asked.

"It's all they had. You want to look for another place?"

I shook my head. "Nothing else between here and Escher. Might as well make do. Dibs on the bed."

Her mouth dropped open. "You shit."

I looked at her. "What?"

"You can't just call the bed."

"I just did," I said.

"But what about chivalry? What about, about…."

"My apartment blew up. I don't have a bed, Ivy. Would you take my bed too? Would you make me sleep in the tub?"

"I… damn you," she said.

"Yes, damn me. In the bed." I stripped my suit jacket and shoes off and hopped on the duvet.

She stood there, mouth agape. Finally, I shot her a grin. I rarely had the chance to get one over on her, so I had to savor those moments when I did. I slid off the bed, pulling the duvet with me. I sketched a little bow and threw it on the floor.

"Your bed awaits, madame."

"Jesus, you're corny."

"That's me," I said, laying on the floor, hands behind my head. "King of the cut-ups, Duke of Yuks."

"Go to sleep."

"Earl of Haha, Emperor of Hilarity, Thane of the Bwahah—"

"Go to sleep, or I will put you to sleep," she threatened.

"But I haven't even gotten to the lesser nobility."

"You're lesser nobility."

"I'll have you know I'm descended from royalty."

"Yeah, the Burger King."

We fell silent for a moment.

"Hey, thanks for this," I said.

No answer came, only the soft steady rhythm of her breathing. I thought again of the things that build a man's fortune and closed my eyes.

———

I woke some time later. The parking lot lights filtered through the gauzy curtains; the hazy buzz of sodium lights the only sound. The dream, or visit, from the night before was still knocking around my head, and I shifted and tossed until I had to sit up. My shoulder ached, as did my arm. I wandered to the bathroom, snagging a bottle of whiskey from Ivy's bag. I'd watched her pack it and knew it was safe. I stripped down and pulled the bandages off. The wounds smelled a little, sharp, like infection. Goddamn devourers.

I poured a measure of whiskey over each, letting it burn its way into the wounds. When I thought the pain might make me black out, I took a swig and did it again, then crawled into the tub. The pain and the booze lowered a shade of melancholy over my heart, and I leaned my head against the cold tile, taking small sips and thinking about recent events.

Ramirez was alive. That was a kick in the gut. The man who'd all but raised me, who taught me to be what I am—alive. The revelation raised more questions than answers. If he was alive, we'd trapped Cory's soul for no reason. And if Cory hadn't killed him, what *had* happened? Was it all smoke and mirrors? To what end? And what was he doing with Gabriel? How had he corrupted her? Why had he turned her on me?

I took another swig of the whiskey. It burned on the way down, then mellowed. My head swam a little.

Had I tortured my former lover for something he had no part in? Or was he just another cog in whatever plan was in motion? How did he keep the secret for so long, and why? And where was the blonde lunatic?

Another slug of whiskey. The room swam. I looked at my ruined hands, and clenched my eyes shut. Regret pounded into my heart like a man with a hammer and no remorse. Tears leaked out, and I did my best to keep the sobs down, but they came anyway.

I didn't notice Ivy until she spoke.

"Jack."

She was sitting on the edge of the tub. She leaned in, took my head in her arms, pulled me close.

"Shh, shh."

I managed to stop sobbing, my chest still hitching. She pulled the bottle from me gently, setting it to the side, then helped me from the tub. We made our way back to the bed, and she climbed in, pulling me after.

"Shh," she said. "It's in the past, Jack. You can't change what happened any more than I can."

Her lips found my forehead, then my cheeks, kissing the tears away. They were soft, warm. They found mine. I tasted the salt of my tears on her lips. Comfort became heat. She rolled onto her back, pulling me atop her, and her hands were pulling at the waistband of my boxers. I kicked them off and she raised her hips, removing her own.

A pause.

"Ivy…" I said.

"Shut up," she replied, and took me into her hand, guiding me inside.

She was hot and wet. I slid inside gently, and she arched her back, my lips finding her nipples. A brief moment of awkwardness as we explored one another, then we fell into a rhythm, all sharp intakes of breath and tensed muscle.

We melted into each other, night turning to dawn turning to morning.

When it was over, we lay back, short of breath, heavy on sweat. Our hands entwined, needing no conversation. In time, sleep came, gentle and heavy.

23

I woke by myself. I lay back, blinking away sleep. I'd been spared dreams for the night, and like a man who'd been on the receiving end of a Marvin Haggler rope-a-dope, could do nothing but sag in relief. The room was quiet, in a way I hadn't known in some time. I could hear the gentle *tick-tick* of the radiator, the hum of the mini-fridge. Even my demons had decided to lay low for the moment.

That sort of quiet rarely comes along anymore. Phones and computers and connected everything—even TVs at gas pumps—all shouting for your attention. If I were a paranoid man, I'd think someone out there doesn't want to give you space to think. But I wasn't. I was just tired, and sore, and for a minute, happy. So, I enjoyed it.

Ramirez was alive. In the sober light of day, the thought hurt less. I started putting pieces together—Cory, Ramirez, Cagliostro, Jacob's girl, the blonde, Gabriel, Praedolor. The names ticked by like the credits to a horror movie. Somehow the old man was planning something. What, I didn't know. But when someone's trying to kill you, the why isn't nearly as important as the how.

He'd likely been in it the whole time with Cory. Likely had been using him as both patsy and henchman.

That felt like an understatement as soon as I thought it. Bad is stubbing your toe and breaking it. This was like sneezing and shitting your heart out.

More importantly, what was I going to do about it? Kill the old man for real? Cory, too? The pragmatic part of me answered without hesitation that I would. The sentimental part... I recalled summer days, the smell of dust and wheat chaff in the barn at Escher's Rest. The old man, his lessons harsh but fair, and always tinged with a little wisdom. Cory, the soft touch of his lips, his crooked smile. Gabriel, that same crooked smile, an edge like a knife that kept things exciting. All these things like hazy sunshine. That pit of worry tightened itself in my stomach, and I rolled onto my side.

The door opened, and Ivy bustled in with two coffees and a paper bag. She gave me a smile, and my guts twisted further. I didn't know yet if we'd tugged the weeds between us out too quickly or not. Even now the blossom might be wilting on the stalk. More things to worry about.

She flopped on the edge of the bed and handed me a coffee, then dug in the bag and passed over a muffin. I made a face.

"Bran? I thought you liked me."

"I can't like you if you drop dead from a bad heart."

"Oh, so you do like me?"

She paused mid-bite, lowered the muffin. "Look, it's... there's a lot of road between here and there."

I nodded, breathed a small sigh of relief. It wasn't a reprieve, but I could deal with a postponement. Hopefully, it'd give me time to untangle my thoughts. Ivy was my best friend. What we'd done—it'd been known to ruin friendships. I didn't want that. I didn't know how she felt, but this seemed like a good indication. A chance to clear our heads a little.

She must've seen something in my expression. "We'll talk after this is over."

"Fair."

I ate the terrible muffin, then cleaned up. When I was dressed, Ivy gave me an appraising look.

"You look a little better today."

"I feel a little better."

She gave me a grin. "Road trip?"

"Road trip," I said.

We left the motel and climbed into her Beamer. It purred to life, and before long, we put the motel and the night before behind us. Something inside berated me for not pushing harder. But I kept a clamp on it for now. I needed a clear head, and that growing warmth in my heart wasn't going to make life easier.

W e were a couple hours in when she broke the silence. "Tell me about Ramirez," she said.

I shrugged, watched the fields pass. "He taught me binding, how to control my demons."

"There's more to it than that."

I sighed and turned my head to watch the oncoming road. "Yeah. He was the closest thing to a father I'd ever had. My own liked to kick me around the way a mean kid will kick a cat. My mother... she had problems of her own. And when my father's raised their ugly head, she took hers out the door. When my dad was finally gone, the next man hated me, too. I used to listen to him talk about how worthless I was through the vents."

Ivy was silent for a minute. "My father died when I was six. My mother had three of us to raise. She did her best. I know what it's like to have that gap in your life. But I never caught the hell you did. I'm sorry, Jack. For what it's worth, you proved them both wrong. You're neither a punching bag nor worthless."

"Yeah, I don't get it. Why would Ramirez do all this unless he'd been broken by a demon? He was always about second chances. Even when I went to prison, he never abandoned me. He encouraged Cory and I to date. When I picked up Gabriel, he even nurtured that relationship. I just can't see him pulling Cory into some conspiracy where he tries to kill you and use me to set a demon free."

Ivy was silent for a long minute. When I looked over, her jaw was clenched. Finally, she spoke.

"That's the hell of it. People change. And not always for the better."

"Can you blame me for hoping otherwise?"

She shook her head. "No. Not at all. I just want you to keep your head."

"Fair enough."

The silence settled between us for a bit. Finally, I reached over and turned the radio on. Kenny Wayne Shepherd was belting out a song. I worried the idea of Ramirez changing, of what could have prompted that. Too many pieces missing. I leaned back and closed my eyes.

T*here was a game I played with my sister called 'Folly'. One person picked three cards from a deck of twenty-one and placed them facedown. The other person had to guess what they were. Getting one correct was a point, two right was five, and all three won you another round. It was named Folly not just because it was a kid's game no adult in their right mind would wager on, but because it was nearly impossible. Our father told us the point of the game was to teach children it was foolish to try to predict the outcome without knowing all the variables. The irony of it was Ellie was a natural. We sometimes played through the whole deck without her missing a beat.*

I placed another card, matching the two I had already laid. We'd just started, but today would be the day. I'd stacked the deck, making sure the order was to my liking, the suits and colors arranged just so—that is to say, I made sure Ellie couldn't know beforehand the lay of the deck. This spread was a Jack, Jack, Queen. I figured she wouldn't be expecting two of the same cards, and if she were, certainly not in spades. I'd thrown the black Queen in there to really throw here, but the more I thought about it, the more I thought that was just kid thinking—imagining any of it as logical.

Ellie sat across from me on the bed, legs tucked under her, and screwed up her face. She closed her eyes and laid a finger on the first card.

"Jack."

Shit.

She moved to the next. "Jack."

Double shit.

I started to sweat a little. I'd been so confident; we'd wagered on this round—I would do her chores for a week if she won. Her finger moved to the last card, and I could tell she was thinking the same thing, a little smirk curling her lips up at the corners.

"Que—"

A crash from downstairs cut her off. Someone was shouting. It ended quickly, and then our mother was crying. Ellie looked at me with wide eyes, the card forgotten.

"Jack—"

I shushed her, my finger to her lips, then leaped off the bed, moving swiftly to the door. I pressed my ear against it. After a moment, I turned back and whispered as loud as I dared.

"Footsteps on the stairs. Hide under the bed."

"What will you do?" She whispered back.

I moved to the chest at the foot of my bed and threw it open, pulling the bat my father had gifted me for my tenth birthday. It was a little short, built for a child, but no less capable of breaking an arm or a leg. I waited beside the door, hand wavering only a little, while Ellie crawled under the bed. She disappeared into the shadows there, and then was

still. Her eyes, wide and staring, peered out at me. A thump on the
stairs, followed by a curse, and I straightened, turning my attention
back to the door.

It burst open, and my father stepped into the room. He took my bat
as one might take candy from a child. I tried to free my arms, but my
father gripped them like a vice. With a snarl, the big man slapped me,
and I fell. Ellie cried out, and our father sneered in her direction then
yanked her from beneath the bed.

She wailed and clawed and bit and thrashed, but it did no good, and
I watched from the floor, dazed and helpless. I stared, as our father
dragged Ellie down the stairs. My vision blurred, and from somewhere
distant, I heard my mother and sister weeping. A tear slid down my
cheek, and the room grew cold.

This is memory.

The world blinked.

This is memory. This is was. This is the thing that has happened,
and I survived. I SURVIVED.

Warmth crept back into my limbs, my body tingling with pins and
needles.

I am the one who lived.

———

When I woke, it was to the BMW slowing, the tires crunching on gravel. I did my best to shake the dreams plaguing me. Reliving the past is bad enough. Like having to go to a smaller Walmart inside a full-size Walmart.

"Bad dream?" Ivy asked.

"Aren't they all?"

She shrugged. "I like puppies. I dream about puppies."

"I'll let my brain know I'd like a solid gold jet next time."

Escher's Rest was at the end of a gravel drive, tucked into a copse of maple, poplar, and oak. We rounded a bend, and the farmhouse came into view. Two stories with an attic dormer, it had one of those porches held up by columns, wide steps leading to the lawn. A swing stood beside the front door.

The barn was just a little past that. Big, red, peaked roof. You know what barns look like. Both were well-kept, Ramirez's estate having left provisions for their maintenance. I think he always hoped I'd take up the trade. Now it seemed he was keeping it for other reasons.

Ivy stopped the car, and we stepped out. She looked between the house and the barn. It was ridiculously nice day, as things go. Gentle breeze, sunshine, bright green everywhere. But I knew the world lied. It'll dress up like a cute little girl in saddle shoes, and as soon as your guard's down, BAM, testicle hockey.

"Which one?" She asked.

I nodded toward the barn. "Binding circle's in there."

We made our way to the barn. It still smelled of chaff and dander and weathered wood. I pushed the door open while Ivy fished a small mason jar out of her bag.

"What's that?" I asked.

"Happy fun time night-night."

She shook it, and glitter swirled in the glass.

"You're evil. Glitter is evil."

"I'm a unicorn, bitch. Now open the door."

I shoved the door open. It slid easily on its track, trundling out of the way. The barn floor was clean and swept, the loft above throwing slanted shafts of sun across the room. I walked over to the iron circle set in the concrete and knelt. The metal was scorched, misshaped in places. I ran my fingers along the edge.

Regnos and Llyrial stirred. Something on the other side took notice, filled my head with a scream like tortured metal. I got a glimpse of wings, blazing white fire. My vision went black, and I clutched my head.

"Jack!" Ivy shouted.

Something heavy landed nearby, and I rolled backwards,

trying to get out of the way. A boot caught me on the point of my hip, and I curled up as it lanced down my leg. I grunted in pain and rolled over to puke. Another boot caught me across the forehead, snapping my head back. My teeth rattled in my skull, and I felt blood pour from my scalp.

"Street smarts!" Ivy shouted.

It was followed by the sound of breaking glass, a yelp of pain, and then a loud *thud*. I rolled away from the puddle of vomit and opened my eyes, blinking them to clear the noise in my head.

When it cleared, I wiped the worst of the blood from my face and looked around. Ivy stood over a bear of a man who was currently laying face-down on the concrete in a puddle of water and glitter.

I staggered to my feet and wandered over, gave him a kick in the ass out of spite.

"Feel better?" Ivy asked.

"I'd feel better if I could pull his teeth out with a tractor," I said.

She laughed. "C'mon, give me a hand. We need to find out who this asshole is."

———

In the history of the world, there have been a few really awful ideas. A land war in Asia. Rock of Ages, starring Tom Cruise. Tying a Russian thug to a chair. The last one was mine. Well, mine and Ivy's.

"Jack. Jack Nyx," Ivy said, snapping my attention back to the man in the chair.

I ground my teeth. Sure, it was fine for her to hide behind an assumed name but using *my* real one was just rude. Especially in front of a man the size of a brick shithouse. He looked up, blinked. I hissed at her and made a cutting motion across my throat.

"Ixnay on the ealray amenay."

She snorted. "I doubt he speaks English, let alone pig Latin, genius."

The big man sneered. "I speak English fine."

"Well, there goes that theory, professor," I snapped at her. I turned back to the big man. "Why are you here?" I asked a little too loud and slow.

He'd kicked me in the head and the hip. I reserved the right to be a dick.

"Fuck you," he said.

I shrugged. "Ivy, hand me the testicle detacher."

His eyes went wide.

"Sorry, the testicle *remover*. Silly English. So hard to get right."

Ivy reached into her pack.

"A man paid me," the Russian said.

"To do what?"

"To make sure you didn't want to be here. Or couldn't be here."

"What'd he look like?" I asked.

The Russian clammed up again.

"Funny expression, clammed up. You know it?" I asked.

He shook his head.

"It's when someone shuts their mouth like a clam. All tight and shit. Well, we have ways of making you talk Mr. Putin."

"My name is Ivan."

"Ivan Putin, right."

"Ivan Ivanovich."

"Wait," Ivy said. "Your name is Ivan son of Ivan? Why not just Ivan the Second?"

"Don't get me started," the big man said.

I glared at them both. "Anyway. Here's how this works. You tell me what the man looked like, or at least his name, and Ivy here will erase your memory."

"I will?"

I shot her another glare. She put on a scowl.

"Of course I will."

"See, then you can't have failed because we don't exist."

"Da, is good."

"So?"

"His name was Ramirez."

"Fuck," I muttered. "Ivy?"

"On it," she said.

She rummaged through a handbag half the size of a Buick and came up with a mason jar full of glitter. She shot me a smile. Six-foot nothing, ebony skin, and eyes you could drown in. It'd be disarming, charming even, if I didn't know the brain behind the smile. She hefted the jar. The Russian had a look on his face that said he was making decisions. Ones we probably wouldn't like.

"Tell me that's memory-erasing dust," I said.

She made a couple passes with the jar, muttering under her breath, then. Her voice rose in volume and the chanting became rhythmic. When it reached its peak, she brandished the jar with a flourish and smashed it over the big man's head, opening a cut at his hairline. He winked out like a cheap light. Glitter exploded everywhere. When it settled, it looked like the room had fallen victim to a vicious pack of scrapbookers.

"Why?" I asked, spitting out tiny metallic flakes. I'd have to have myself declared a superfund site.

She shrugged and picked up her handbag. Somehow, she'd managed to escape even a flake of glitter. She shouldered past me on the way to the door.

"Not everything has to have a magical solution, you know. Sometimes I just like to fuck with you."

Witches.

I paused at the door. A small statue sat on the floor. I picked it up, turned it in my hands.

"What's this?" I asked.

Ivy stopped, gave it a look, then a shrug.

"Tchotchke."

"Tchotchke?"

"Yeah, knick-knack."

"I know what a tchotchke is."

"Then why'd you ask?"

I growled in frustration and tossed it over my shoulder, then followed her out. Ivy waited beside the Beamer with an impatient tilt to her eyebrow. I glanced back at the barn. My gut knotted, and I worried my lip with my teeth.

"Tell me you did *something* to his memory," I said.

She fished her keys from a pocket and tapped the start. The BMW purred to life.

"Relax, of course I did something. I'm a smartass, not an idiot. I don't need Ivan Strongmeat there coming after me, either."

I relaxed a fraction, my shoulders unknotting enough to ease the headache already crawling up the back of my skull. She paused, the door to the car half-open.

"You did get the thing, right?" She asked.

"Thing?" I asked.

"Proof. If Ramirez is really doing this, we need proof. It's got to be somewhere around here."

"I thought you got the thing."

"Jack."

"Yeah?"

"We came here for the thing."

"Yeah."

"Well, I don't have the thing. And you don't have the thing…"

"Fuck."

"Yes, fuck. Go get the thing."

I swore again.

I was halfway to the house when the barn door exploded from the frame. Most people use that word in a hyperbolic way. "My head exploded": *I was shocked.* "My ears exploded": *It was loud.* "My stomach exploded": *I chased tacos with coffee.*

In this case, the door exploded into a cloud of splinters and wooden shards, and a bear the size of a small fucking truck exited the building. It was covered in glitter. And it was *pissed.*

"Jack!" Ivy shouted from behind me. "Bear!"

I was too busy running toward the car, which she had already climbed into and shut tight, but if I wasn't, I expect my response would have been something witty like "Thanks!", or "No shit!", or maybe "Fuuuuuuuuuck!". As it was, my lungs were too busy trying to suck air as I put on speed. Not enough of it though. Bears are really hard to outrun, a fact I wish I'd paid more attention to in class.

I heard the bear's paws pounding on the gravel—closer, closer —it blasted out a growl that would've emptied my guts if I'd eaten anything recently. Its breath smelled like vodka and beef jerky. I did not want to join those smells.

Something parted the air behind me, and I let out a manly squeal. I put on a touch more speed. Ivy's face was illuminated by the car's dash, and I saw her take something from her purse—I didn't have time to look, but a spark of hope lit my chest. I had to buy her time.

I skidded to a halt and spun. The bear was even bigger up close.

"Let's investigate, Jack. You need the peace of mind, Jack. Ever been fucked by a bear, Jack?" I muttered, fear fueling my senseless yammering.

I called on Regnos, and rage filled me, strength flooding my limbs, my skin hardening. It made it difficult to move, but I didn't plan on running for at least five more seconds. And if it went wrong, plenty of people lived full lives without legs.

The bear reached me and lunged forward, jaws open. I threw a hard-right hook into its snout. It recoiled, head snapping to the side, and yowled in pain. Regnos roared approval, urging me to press the attack, and I surged forward, landing a left jab into its eye.

You like that, you furry circus reject? Regnos taunted in my head. The bear reared up, and I realized I'd made a tactical mistake. Bears are big. This was an extra big bear. So, when a twelve-foot tall bear swats you with a paw the size of a Thanksgiving turkey, physics takes over, muscle and hardened skin be damned.

I flew. Not like a bird, but like a man who's been thrown by a bear. Thankfully, a tree was there to break my fall. I felt several somethings crack. A flash of light, and a scream. Gobbets of the bear erupted into the sky, showered the bucolic scene.

Ivy rushed over, kneeling beside me. She rummaged in her bag and started to smear something on my hip. It smelled like horseradish. It wasn't erotic. I didn't complain. The statue stood next to her. The bear was gone, replaced with the remains of the Russian. From where I lay, I caught a glimpse of a leg hanging in a tree.

I blinked and looked up at Ivy. "I won."

She scoffed. "Please. I won."

I groaned as pain crept back into my body. She made soothing sounds and finished rubbing the smelly lotion on me.

"Thanks," I said.

"Try to stay still. It takes a bit to work."

"Good. I need a nap."

I lay back in the grass and closed my eyes for a bit.

Having your brain knocked around the inside of your skull like it's a pinball machine played by a gorilla on its last quarter tends to kick some things loose.

Maybe it was an object lesson. Maybe it was the lie of time, digging up old memory just to hurt me, and that old nightmare of prison knocked on the door, begging to be let in, but as Ivy's medicine did its work, my mind drifted.

I woke for the third time that morning, to a room full of the dead.

They stood in packed rows, from wall to wall, and stared at me in mute expectation. I sat up, and stared back, unsure of what to do. A part of me knew I should be afraid, this was the thing the other inmates had tried to key me into. The thing was, even looking at them up close, even in the face of the event, I found the whole situation mostly unbelievable.

Instead, I did what came naturally. I voided my bladder in the combination toilet and sink set into the wall, brushed my teeth, and washed my face. When I finished, I made my way back to my bunk, pushing past men who had been burned, stabbed, strangled, and electrocuted. I saw others with obvious gunshot wounds, raw and sucking, and others with clear signs of frostbite, or head injuries. A veritable cornucopia of death. I took all of this in and sat back down.

Still, they stared at me. There didn't seem to be a leader, but they had come to me for a reason, and I suspected only time would tell what that thing might be. I closed my eyes to avoid their gaze and tried to think.

Nothing came right away, and I found myself listening to the silence instead. It was cool, and patient, and gave nothing back. I opened my eyes, still trying to think of anything but the dead, and found the cell empty. Down the hall, a buzzer sounded, and cell doors clicked open. Inmates shuffled by on their way to breakfast, and as soon as my door popped, I followed.

I grabbed breakfast, a tray of toast and fruit and a bowl of oatmeal and sat down with Croft and Dimes. I looked around for a moment, then frowned.

"Where's Tucker?" I asked.

Croft ducked his head and took a big mouthful of oatmeal. Dimes shrugged.

"Dunno man."

I looked around the mess, trying to see if anyone else was missing. Carter and Alan, it looked like. Maybe others. I frowned again, then *shrugged it off. It was Coldhaven. It was common knowledge the place would eat you alive if you let it. From solitary to violence, there wasn't a scrap of soul the cold walls wouldn't try to get a taste of.*

We ate in silence for a while, keeping our thoughts private. It wasn't long before my thoughts turned to the dead, and why they had come for me. I thought maybe they wanted something, though asking a dead guy what he wants out loud is a lot like wanting to end up in a padded cell.

I entertained the thought maybe I was seeing the dead now because something had changed. Maybe the stress of the place was getting to me, and it was my mind that slipped, like cheese off a cracker. I saw it on the faces of the men I knew. Everyone was drawn tight as piano wire. Life wasn't getting any easier.

Dimes broke the silence. "You know what I miss, man?"

He spooned a glob of oatmeal up, and lifted his spoon, then turned it over, letting the grey goop fall back into the bowl with a plop. "Burgers."

Croft snorted, and I even caught myself smiling. I was still smiling when I saw one of the dead men from my cell standing behind the serving line, a thin line of red etched across his throat. I felt the smile slip from my face and hid it by taking a bite of toast. The ghost stared for a moment more, then faded from view.

"Heh. Burgers." Croft nudged me, but my sense of humor had fled.

I finished breakfast, bussed my tray, and left. Behind my, I could just barely make out Dimes asking Croft what had crawled up my ass.

———

I *stopped by my cell and changed into sweats and running shoes, then made my way to the yard. Outside, the grass was a pale yellow, and the few trees in sight held orange and brown leaves. Overhead, clouds lay in their beds, the gray of weathered wood, their undersides blue-black and threatening. The air was just this side of bitter, and I drew the hood of my pullover tight, and made my way to the dirt track marked out on the far side of the yard.*

I took a breath, and began to run, feet pounding in a regular rhythm matching my heartbeat and breathing for a while. This early, the yard was still far from full, and I had the track to myself. For a while, I enjoyed the solitude and the near silence. I let the rhythm of the run lull me into a relaxed state and did my best not to worry over the haunts.

It was probably my sixth time around when I saw the first of the spectators, the dead man from the mess. He was standing on the side of the track, watching me run. I made another lap, and instead of fading, another man appeared, then another. For each lap, more men flickered into view, their eyes dead and silent.

I veered from the track at the last minute and began to sprint toward the double doors leading to the cellblock, and away from the dead silence behind me. On my way in, I nearly knocked over Markham, and had to jag at a sharp angle to avoid the guard. For a moment, it looked like he was going to reach out and knock me on my ass, but he let me pass, and then I was inside, away from the dead and the sadistic guard.

I stood just inside the doors, breathing hard for a minute, heart thudding in my chest like a runaway kettledrum. When I had it under control, I headed back to my cell, and collapsed on my bunk. My brain tried to make sense of what was happening, but all it could seem to tell me was what I already knew, like the world's shittiest newscaster.

The dead had come for me.

———

T hree hours later found me working in the laundry, a cavernous room full of industrial size washers and driers, and the ever-present hum of machinery. It was hot there, probably ten to twenty degrees more than on the block and sweat condensed on me as though I were being dunked every few minutes.

My work section was a bit away from the others. I'd been there long enough they trusted me without constant supervision and let me work the machines alone. I tossed another load into a dryer, slammed the door shut, and fired it up. The laundry began to spin and thump against the *inside. I turned to fill the washer with another load when I found himself face to face with the dead again. They stood in ranks on ranks, and their eyes looked desperate.*

The one in front, a man with a burn on his face, and blood crusted around his eyes, grabbed me, and it was cold. I struggled, but it was too late. Others pressed against me as well, and one by one, they bore me to the floor. A piece of metal—probably the shiv I kept hidden under the soap ledge—glittered in the light, and a sock was shoved in my mouth. I felt the blade bite and tug at my skin, and I screamed, but it was already muffled.

It seemed the pain went on forever, and when it was over, there was another, another dead man with the blade, etching something into my flesh. I bled, and I struggled, and I screamed, but eventually, the pain and the fear took me and throttled me, and I blacked out.

———

I woke in black waves washing out from behind my eyes, lightening to pink, and then yellow. Dull pain washed across my skin, and I felt bindings wrapping me tight. Beside me, I heard someone speaking in a low voice.

"Thirteen are they, cold in the heavens, and upon the deep. Dead they are, yet living, they reap the wheat and shake the chaff. In the sky, their stars shake the foundations and tear the firmament. Thirteen are they, black upon the world, the promise of life everlasting."

I cracked my eyes. Markham stood beside the bed, head down, bad hand clasped over his good one. One of my own arms was uncovered. Red marks scrawled across the flesh cut into my skin. I looked back up at Markham, who still stood with his head bowed and decided to play possum until the man left.

After another moment of silence, he walked from the room. I opened my eyes fully and lifted my arm to peer at the cuts in my skin. They were raw—but clean, and the closer I looked, the easier it was to make out the symbols and figures cut there.

The language seemed to shift, the symbols reminiscent of something I'd seen before, but like most vague memories, it played coy. I wondered what the dead had done, what misery had driven them to this. I thought of the men of the prison, and the torment in their lives. I thought of all the unfinished business, of the misery left behind.

I dropped my arm. The dead had carved their intent into my flesh, marking me like a ledger of wrongs done by the world. I pulled back the sheet. The bandages only covered my torso and arms. Relief they had chosen to stop there flooded me, despite the ache throbbing through me.

The doc, an old man with sharp eyes, a sharp nose, and a clipboard pulled the curtain around my bed aside. He checked the board, then gave me a once-over, measuring me.

"How are you feeling?" he asked.

"Like ten miles of shit road, doc."

The doctor nodded and made a mark on his board. "Any idea who did this to you?"

"You think I'd tell even if I did?"

The doc shook his head. "Didn't think so. Well, Mr. Nyx, you're free to go this afternoon. You're a bit carved up, and you lost some blood, but keep your wounds clean, and come in every other day to swap out the bandages, and you should be fine. I'll have the nurse bring you something for the pain shortly."

I nodded. "Thanks, doc."

The doctor left, and I sank back into the bed. I wondered what Markham's sudden interest meant, and what the strange prayer signified. I closed my eyes and waited for the nurse to bring me something to dull my brain.

———

I ran into Dimes on the way back to the block. I was wearing my khakis again, and the bandages only showed on my arms and to the base of my neck.

"Holy shit, Nyx. What happened to you?" He asked.

"Fell into a blender."

"No shit?" Dimes quirked an eyebrow. "Someone shove you in a dryer?"

I shook my head. "Just an accident, that's all."

"Hell of an accident. Well, feel better, man." Dimes went to walk past me, and even raised a hand to pat me on the shoulder. He seemed to think better of it though and dropped it mid-raise. "Feel better."

I continued, back to my cell. I didn't feel up to spending time in the day room, where the TV would be blaring, men would be playing cards and chess, and everyone gathered would feel the need to ask what happened or stare. I went inside and lay on my bunk. After some time, I drifted off again.

———

When I woke again, it was past dark, and my stomach was rumbling. I'd slept through dinner. I sat up in my bunk and grabbed a package of cheese crackers from the shelf. Thank God for the commissary. I ate in silence, and when I finished, washed it down with a cup of water from the in-room sink.

The hall on the block was silent aside from the occasional snore or cough, and I sat in bed, staring up at the ceiling. I was trying to work out all that had happened when the sound of footsteps and the odd jangle of keys pulled me from my head.

Markham was on the other side of the door, staring in. Something glittered in his hand, and I leaned forward until his face was inches from the bars.

"We need to talk, boy."

With his good hand, he inserted a key into the lock, and pushed it to the side, just enough to let himself in. I glanced down at the thing in his mangled hand and saw with little surprise that it was a blade, about four inches long. Its edge glittered in the low light. When it rains, it's usually shit.

I pushed myself against the wall and looked around for a way to defend myself. Too late though, and Markham was close.

"You have no business holding those names, boy. They're owed to me."

I drew a blank and tried to think of some defense. Nothing came out. Markham raised the knife and slashed down once. I was able to get my arm up in time to block the blow, but the blade cut through the bandages easily, and into my arm. I felt fresh blood well up, hot and wet, and my stomach quavered.

Markham brought the blade up again. Again, I was able to stop it with my arm, but another hot line of fire traced its way down my flesh, and I winced in agony. I cast about the room, looking for a way out, but saw none. I wondered if the stress was going to stop my heart and finish this for Markham.

In the corner, something moved, and I saw the face of a dead man. The light shifted as Markham paced away from me, his rage sated for a moment, and I saw a second specter in the corner. There was a feeling in the air, as though someone held their breath, waiting. I looked down at my arm and saw the knife slashes had crossed out two of the symbols cut there.

"Who are you that the Thirteen should deem you worthy?" Markham asked, his face half in shadow. I could hear the rage still in his voice. He tilted his head up and asked the ceiling. "Who is this pup?"

With Markham distracted, I took my chance and grabbed the can of tuna I'd stashed on my shelf, ripping the pull-tab off. The edge came away sharp and wicked in the half-light. The stink of tuna filled the air. I hadn't imagined this for a death.

Markham's head turned at the pungent smell of fish in the cell and quirked a smile. "You hungry, bitch? Maybe you'd like some fresh-cut meat?"

I didn't answer. Instead, I gritted my teeth against the promise of pain, and began to slash at my arms with the can lid, opening new wounds. I cut and cut, and Markham stopped in his tracks and watched, half amused, half baffled.

"What the fuck? Doing my job for me?"

"You'll. See." I said through a grimace and cut again.

Behind Markham, the crowd of the dead grew with each cut, with each name crossed off the list. With a final slash, I drew the lid across my chest. I hoped this worked. I hurt everywhere, and the floor of the cell was getting slick.

For a moment, nothing happened, and Markham raised the blade again. Then the dead began to move. They first put tentative hands on the old officer, then more aggressively as they discovered they could touch him. He paused mid-act, unable to move as the dead began to weigh him down. A few moved in front of him, to grab him by the shoulders from that side, or the chest.

Then the dead began to pull. For a moment, nothing happened. Then there was a pop, like a gun going off, and one of his arms hung limp in its socket. Markham screamed. It didn't stop the dead. They pulled and pulled, until fabric and flesh ripped and tore, until blood and entrails and gore covered the floor. They pulled until the man was fully dead, and his screams stopped echoing in the halls.

When the other guards came, they found a bloody mess, and an exhausted inmate. I smiled at them, and tossed the tuna lid to the side, while the dead watched. For a long time, the guards stood at the entrance to the cell, and no one said anything.

I finally broke the silence.

"Anyone got a band-aid?"

———

I woke, blinked the sleep from my eyes, and shook the dregs of the dream. It hadn't happened that way. I'd never killed Markham. He was two hundred pounds of sadism, and I did my best to fly under the radar, so I didn't spend a month in the infirmary with a broken leg. I didn't like to think of him. Something was fucking with my dreams. I'd blame it on the head trauma, but that was almost always consistent.

My head ached, my body less so, despite being punched by a bear and laying on a barn floor. I sat up and groaned, then pressed the heels of my hands against my eyes until I saw stars in an effort to calm the throbbing there.

Whatever I'd seen when I'd touched the circle lay behind them, and I knew then the meaning of the dream and the vision. I let my hands drop and looked around for Ivy. She sat against the open barn door, watching.

When I looked up, she gave me a smile.

"How're you feeling?"

I stood, groaning again. Lifted my shirt. I was covered in bruises fading from black to green, and a little oily from her ointment.

"Not as bad as I'd expect. What was that stuff?"

She stood to join me, offered me her shoulder. "Ben-Gay by witches. It'll keep you together for a couple days, but you'll need to see a doctor before too long." She was quiet as we limped to the house. She set me on the swing on the porch. "You need to slow down before you end up dead."

I nodded. "Just a few more days, and I'll take a vacation, I promise. Right now, I just want a drink."

She was quiet again. Finally, she nodded, changed the subject. "Think the water's still running?"

I chuckled. "The old man was anal. I guarantee it's running. Probably lights, too."

"Be right back."

She disappeared into the house. I sat on the swing and rocked a little. Aside from the severed limb hanging in a tree, the country night was peaceful. Crickets and bullfrogs sang nearby. The stars looked like a handful of mica someone had scattered across velvet. The trees rustled and whispered, telling one another secrets as a breeze rippled the grass and cooled my skin.

Ivy's voice came from the kitchen.

"Jack!"

I groaned once more for good measure and stood, making my way inside. The door opened silently, the screen door clattering against the frame behind me. My past battered against me as soon as I broke the threshold.

The smell of Brut—the old man had never had the best taste in cologne—and stale cigars. The yellow-white linoleum and green cabinets. The kitchen table with its chrome trim, and the chipped laminate by the sink where pots had been banged into it. The divide between the kitchen and deep shag carpet in the hall, a cheap metal strip nailed in place to hide the demarcation. In all, it looked like an interior decorator had mugged the 70s and strewn its bell-bottom clad corpse across a fifteen-foot square crime scene.

Ivy stood over the table, a fist on her hip. I limped over. The surface of the table had been covered with arcane symbols; the Enochian there crude but effective. An empty jar sat in the middle of the circle. I trudged up the hall, already knowing what I'd find.

The living room had been desecrated as well, the couches and recliner long gone, the carpet torn up, exposing particle board subfloor. Another circle had been carved there, and great splotches of dried blood marred the pale surface.

Ivy called from down the hall. "Jack. Don't come in here."

She was in my old room. I resisted the impulse to go anyway. She came back out, pale as a black woman can get. My stomach dropped.

"It's the girl."

She nodded, and Regnos peeked her head up. That was their game. They'd needed an innocent for their ritual. The girl was the key. My stomach turned. Angels aren't above accepting sacrifice. The Bible's full of it. They'd bled the girl to make the pact, and now angels were possessing Vessels, and it was driving them insane.

"At least we know what happened with Cory," I said.

"This is where they put his soul into a body?" She asked.

I nodded. "Yeah, but someone had to lose theirs."

"Which means..."

"It means they probably fed that poor sap's soul to lure Praedolor out so they could bind it. And they used the girl to make a pact with the angels."

"What the fuck are they up to, Jack?"

"I'm not sure yet, but if I were prone to understatement, I'd say it's not great."

I left the living room, and stomped out of the house, onto the porch. I stood there, taking deep breaths of fresh night air. Some things will knock the wind out of you as sure as a punch in the gut. I breathed deep and heavy, until I was calm, until Regnos settled down. Even Xiphos was beginning to stir. The demons wanted blood, and I didn't blame them. The door closed behind me, and Ivy joined me.

"What now?" She asked.

"I've got a city to talk to."

"Interesting."

"Not really."

We made our way to the BMW.

"You have the weirdest friends," Ivy said.

"Nice self-burn," I said as we pulled out.

"You wanna walk? Because that's how you end up walking."

"I rescind my statement. Onward, Jeeves."

"Boy, I will stab you with these keys."

I laughed despite myself and flipped the radio on. Creedence kicked on, and the highway rolled past.

24

There's a church on 4th. I stay away from it for the most part, since I'd cut ties with the network. It's a quaint thing, older than most of the city, but well-kept with a big worship room thingy (seriously, churches are anathema to my feeling not like shit), and a steeple that's in the Goldilocks zone. Not too tall, not too short. Just right, in other words.

But the main reason I don't go is because it's one of the few places that's actually connected. These big churches, these near-corporate undertakings with their Joel Osteen ostentatiousness—there's an insincerity to them. Like lip service Catholics. Eat the wafer, drink the wine, go back to pounding your secretary on Monday.

Here though, there's a sincerity of faith that's inarguable. Someone here, and by extension, their congregation, are believers. And that's dangerous for people like me. But it's also the only way to talk to the people who matter. As soon as we got back to town, I asked Ivy to run an errand. Life had told me to listen to my hunches, and I needed her to track one down. Besides, I figured I could have a conversation on my own. Which left me sitting in a pew, talking to a plaster Jesus.

"Life is a spiral for most people. In and in and in, the center just out of reach. If you do reach the middle, you're generally better off not having done so, because there's a minotaur there, and he's an asshole. The minotaur is a metaphor, of course. For... death? Yeah, that sounds right.

"Look, you want philosophy? Ask Plato. He's up there, right? Or maybe not. Was he the guy that drank the hemlock?

"Where was I?

"Oh, yeah...

"My life follows a similar path, except someone tipped the spiral on its side, and it's mostly periods of climbing against a stubborn arc just to fall like a rock down the other side. On the upside, the minotaur probably has a terrible case of motion sickness. Sure, you can take the spider-lady's advice—tie a string to one end so you can find your way back, but how many of us want to do that? I can think of roughly fifteen years I'd rather not relive thanks to dear ol' dad."

I was really feeling my monologue now.

"That's not fair. Sure, he was an asshole. Sure, he believed in the policy of the closed fist over the open hand, and if his hands were full, he believed in the language of a thick leather belt from JC Penney. Still, the demons came early for me, and they weren't entirely his fault. I can't say they were my mother's fault either, though when she saw the storm coming, more often than not, she left me to weather it alone. The rest, well, loneliness can wreak havoc on a guy's life. Or maybe it was a curse, some sort of centuries-old familial faux pas leaving the seventeenth generation with a shitty door prize.

"All this is to say I don't really know where the demons come from. But I'm stuck with them.

"Why am I telling you this?"

I turned to the plaster Jesus His eyes uplifted to heaven as if caught rolling them in perpetuity. He was crucified in the usual way, that is to say, painfully, and the crown of thorns hung crooked over one eye as if the artist had originally wanted to sculpt a fedora on there and had a fight with the church, and this is what they got instead after a great deal of hemming and hawing and muttering about vision. I watched him for a beat more, and when he didn't reply, stood from the pew. That's when the blood started to flow.

I'm not sure how He did it, or why He'd chosen me to speak to on those infrequent occasions. When an avatar of a god, writhing and impaled and bleeding on the pulpit spoke, you listened, or you found out there were worse things than demons.

He shifted His head toward me with a cracking sound, the plaster just loose enough to allow Him to crane His neck. His eyes rolled in their sockets, and blood streamed and pattered from His wounds. He opened dry lips—part of me wondered if it was sacrilege to give a plaster Jesus a drink from the sacramental wine—and spoke.

"753 54th."

"Is that a verse?"

The statue moaned and twisted, snapping one of His arms free from the crucifix. I shut the hell up. Thinking snarky is one thing. Taunting a god—regardless of denomination—was an incredibly good way to get a limb ripped off and shoved in a tight, sensitive area. Peace and love my ass, most of these guys were all about righteous fury.

"753 54th. Anne Hamilton."

I nodded, and the statue moved one last time, arm going back to the outstretched position, face turned up. It ceased moving and bleeding, and I blew a breath out. I stood there for a moment with my head bowed. I wasn't worried about being caught talking to a plaster Jesus, but I was worried about *looking* like I was. That's the sort of thing that earns you a trip to your friendly psych ward, and an all-expenses paid three-day nap courtesy of Halidol.

I left the church, passing a priest on my way out. He stopped me.

"Are you well, child?"

I nodded and hooked a thumb over my shoulder. "Yeah, but that guy could use a drink. Maybe think about forgetting to put the wine away next communion."

I stepped out, still thinking about the implications of a god getting drunk on transubstantiation.

———

You've got two choices when a god gives you a directive. Procrastinate or crusade. I'm not exactly the Joan of Arc type, so I sat in a diner on 45th and watched my eggs congeal over a rapidly cooling cup of coffee. Besides, you know how Joan ended up. Being tied to stakes and set on fire is against my religion.

The waitress stopped by and topped off my coffee with a smile. I had to squash Llyrial's response. Desire stirred in my stomach, and my heartbeat sped up. For a moment, I imagined the two of us locked in the broom closet, sweating off the toast. I pushed it away. One thing you can say about demons. They're impulsive. And kind of stupid. And mean.

Okay, that's three things, but they *can* be useful. Mainly, I just tried to keep them in line, a trick that in the past had involved self-medication and isolation. These days, the arcane circles on my arms bound them to me and kept their exploits to a dull roar. Downside, they bound them to me. I mean, demons with you all the time is the ultimate baggage. Forget heavy social drinking, trust issues, or a gambling addiction. I had half the deadly sins etched into my flesh.

This felt different somehow. I'd been given a name. Which meant either someone was in deep shit, and I was screwing them over while gnawing on reheated Jimmy Dean sausage, or there was more going on here than I could see at the time. I really hoped it was the second. The idea of leaving someone alone with a demon made my stomach do Red Baron loops in my gut.

Anxiety finally made the decision for me, and I paid the bill and left a tip, walking into the day. Llyrial nudged me again, putting the picture of the waitress and I in my brain, her body contorted in pleasure. I nudged back with a snarl and squashed it. I ignored the guilt riding shotgun, trying not to speculate about how Ivy might feel about those thoughts. When the cashier jumped, I turned the sound into a cough.

"Sorry," I half-smiled.

She gave me a look suggesting I belonged anywhere but there and gave me my change. Another successful social interaction. I left quicker than I'd planned, but at least no one was whipping waffles at my head.

———

I stood in front of the home at 753 54th, nursing my guilt. I felt terrible for even thinking the things I had earlier. When you're carrying demons, guilt is a constant companion. I imagine it's like reliving a Catholic childhood every other hour. I shrugged it to the back of my mind, where I could pull it out and obsess over it later and checked out the house.

It was a skinny white thing in a district filled with skinny white things. Neat siding, neat windows, neat porch. The door was Christmas green, and the porch a deep burgundy, and I suspected the owner might be demented, probably by gentrification. I sucked air between my teeth, stepped up, and knocked. You'd think a guy wouldn't knock on the door of a possibly demon-haunted house, but manners are underrated, and besides, if I walked in and the homeowner had a gun, I was gonna be pissed if someone shot me.

No answer came, so I knocked again, hard, and stepped back,

eyeing the window. I could break it, but again, I'm allergic to bullets, so until I knew the place was definitely empty, I wasn't breaking into shit. Thankfully, I heard someone shuffling around inside, and a moment later, the door opened. The scent of roast beef wafted out.

The woman who opened the door was much like her house. Skinny and white, her hair pulled back. She wore an oversized sweater and leggings, and her face was hard angles and big eyes. She looked like the sort of person who was perpetually disappointed, and likely never missed the chance to tell someone so.

"Yes?" She said, her face indicating she thought I might smell like poor.

"Anne Hamilton?"

"And you are?"

"Jack." I waited for the question—last name? Everyone wants to know. I tell them it's like Madonna, or Prince. Just Jack.

Instead, her eyes wrinkled at the corners as though some bit of understanding had bored its way into her consciousness, and she smiled, the change as unexpected and sudden as a break in a storm.

"Oh, it's you. Come in."

My gut twisted at the change, sending up warning signals like a lumberjack who's suddenly realized he's about to drop a tree on a baby. Look, it's not the best metaphor, but there are only so many ways of saying I suspected shit was about to get knee-deep. Still, a lead's a lead, and I stepped inside.

The interior of the house was as neat as the exterior, all clean lines, doilies, and hardwood. I thought Martha Stewart might be jealous, if not enraged that this lady was stealing her schtick. The smell of meat cooking was pleasant but not overpowering, and my stomach rumbled.

She led me to a couch in a well-lit sitting room, and took a wingback chair across from me, crossing her legs as the ankles. If she extended her pinky, I had plans to jump out the window. She offered a cup of tea from the tray beside her. I took it and sipped. It was good. Better than the Earl Grey I drank sometimes. To be honest, that stuff tasted like my grandma's sweaters smell. This was pleasant in comparison.

She smiled. "They told me you'd come."

"Who?"

"The demons."

My heart did a skip-beat, and I tensed. I reached for my own passengers, giving them a nudge. This was bad. Ghostbusters 2 bad. She laid a hand on my arm, her touch warm and soft. My instinct was to shake it off. I wasn't a fan of being touched, even by those close to me. A lifetime of walking on eggshells will do that.

"No need for that dear," she said. "Not yet, anyway."

She sat back, and I hesitated. She continued to sip her tea, and I sank back into the chair. I had questions. For her, and for me. Did she really talk to demons? Was I sent here to help or end her? Maybe she was nuttier than squirrel shit. And finally, what was in that roast? It smelled like heaven.

"What do you want? Wait—scratch that. Is that the mailman in the oven, because he smells delicious." I was trying to goad her because I'm stupid like that.

She laughed, a light tinkling sound. "Just a roast, Jack. And I just want to talk."

"About what?"

"About your demons."

"So, when you said the demons told you…"

"I meant it. I have mine. Everyone does, Jack. They crawl around in your brain and make your thoughts wrong. The trick is owning them, not the other way around."

"Mine are under control."

"Are they?"

I thought back to the images running in my head from earlier. I shrugged. "Most of the time."

"What if I told you they could be gone?"

"You didn't get rid of yours."

"I don't need to."

"Neither do I."

"Don't you? How many did you hurt before you got 'control' of yours? How many times did you hurt yourself?"

A girl met in the rain; the relationship tempestuous. To the point it led to prison—modern day Bonnie and Clyde. I spent four years pacing those concrete floors, my soul drained by the dim gray. Partner after partner, each relationship broken on the rocks. An inability to hold a job. Drugs. Each of these things like a rock thrown into a bucket of water, raising the level until it overflowed the lip.

And then I met the man who first talked me through the fire, and then showed me the circles. One for Llyrial, Scion of Lust. One for Regnos, Scion of Rage. One for Xiphos, Scion of Death. And finally, finally, I had an outlet, thanks to control. I was given a purpose, thanks to a god who still needed lust and rage and madness.

I thought about it. I thought about inappropriate relationships, about rage threatening to spill over into violence, about insignificant words turned into hateful slights and feelings of abandonment. I thought about lust and the places it had taken me unchecked by reason.

I thought about all the people I had hurt, and the times I had hurt, and she had a point. But it was a moot point. I had taken those things and wrapped them in my fist and used them to punch my life in the face until it acted right. I wasn't going back. I had earned my gifts.

"No," I said.

She set her teacup down, and her face darkened. The temperature in the room dropped a few degrees. Literally. I could see my breath. She stood and pushed up the sleeves of the sweater. Every inch of her forearms were covered in circles, and as she ran her hands over them, they lit up like a Christmas tree.

"Arrogant," she said, and kicked her chair back. It flew into the wall, smashing the drywall there. "Stupid." She flung the tea tray, scattering china in a glass tinkle, and embedding the silver platter in the wall.

Part of me agreed with her. Part of me didn't want to hit a girl. Part of me didn't think it mattered, because she had me by my shirt collar and was tossing me as easily as the chair. I flew through the air in much the way men aren't supposed to and smashed into the wall. One of my knees made a sound like a piece of bubble wrap going off. I normally like that sound. This one made me puke as pain lanced upward into my guts. I sincerely hoped I hadn't shattered the kneecap.

There are three moments every man remembers in his life. His first kiss, his first car, and the first time a ninety-pound woman is smashing your face into a hardwood floor. I think it was oak. It tasted like oak.

She was on my back, using my head like a mallet, and the hardwood was out of place. I tried to roll, and instead earned a kidney punch. My back spasmed, and I tasted blood. Those were probably my teeth trying to run away, like the rest of me wanted to.

She let up for a moment, picking me up by my shirt. She stared me in the eyes, her pupils red. "You. Hurtful. Greedy. Weak. What you can't give up must be taken from you. You will be cleansed. War it is, and the world will be better for it."

She slammed me into the wall, and my back spasmed again. When I got out of this, I was going to send the church my chiropractor bill. I managed to get enough of my senses about me, grabbing hold of my own demons just as she pinned me again, hips grinding into mine as she landed a right hook on my jaw.

I felt her pushing lust onto me, her own demon throwing out suggestion and pheromones. I arched my back, throwing her off as the first of Regnos' strength flooded into me. She tumbled off in a backward somersault and came up on her feet. It was like fighting Mary Lou Retton on PCP.

I stood, trying to blink away the bleariness in my vision, but she was already moving, a low growl rumbling in her chest. Fear and desperation shot my fist out and it connected. Her head snapped back, and I felt her nose crinkle under the impact. She reeled back, spitting blood and curses.

"Shit! Sorry! Sorry!" Guilt wracked me. She didn't care. She moved in, grabbing my arm, and doing some sort of flip bending it in the wrong direction. It held for a moment, then with a *pop*, blew out of the socket. I screamed and hit my knees, and that brought another garbled moan of pain. My arm hung at a weird angle, like a windshield wiper someone pulled out of its mount. I felt Regnos' strength bleed from me.

She stood over me for a moment, then smirked. With a quick turn of her heel, she disappeared into the kitchen. I hoped she was bringing me a plate of roast beef. When she showed up with a knife, I still hoped it was to cut the roast beef. She pressed a foot into my chest, flipping me back, then sat on my hips.

"You couldn't just say yes," she said. She dragged the knife down my cheek, and I felt a hot line of blood and pain follow it. I did the only thing left. I called on Xiphos. Rage and lust and love and hate and sorrow and fear and joy all flooded me, over-whelming my senses. The world flickered and went dark for a time.

---

he farmhouse trickled in, black fading to color washed as if water had diluted the vision. We were upstairs, me and Ellie, huddled in our bedroom, beds pushed against the wall, a shared dresser between us. The window beside me showed the fields, broken stalks rising from now-fallow ground, that the harvest season had passed.

They were brown and yellow, the color of the wasps hanging around the eaves of the barn. I remembered my father, burly and covered with hair like a Cossack, swearing and swatting at them with a shovel, dowsing them with gasoline as they hit the ground, firing their delicate paper walls. The wasps would boil out, their voices like small thunder, but he would just laugh at them, wrapped in thick canvas and his beekeeper's helmet.

That's what it sounded like now, small thunder, only not as distant, as our father rumbled at our mother, the sounds angry, like spears tipped with lightning. I could hear her, my mother's voice tiny, a frightened doe in the rain, mostly weeping, but occasionally issuing denials in small cloudbursts. My hands trembled, and I looked over at Ellie. She had buried herself in her blankets, only hir eyes peeping out. We said nothing, but each shared the same thought. The sound downstairs had tapered, and we looked toward our door, and the general direction of the stairs, hope in our eyes, and then it came, more thunder, loud this time, our father bellowing in rage. It cracked against the walls and splashed into our heads like lightning against water. A pause, and then another—

———

W hen I found myself again, it was to the sounds of my own weeping. There are some moments that never leave you. Some things that are a part of you, no matter how hard you try to fight. Anne, or the thing that had been wearing Anne's skin, laid crumpled in the corner, the blade protruding from her chest. She stared upward, her Martha Stewart clothing and her Martha Stewart house looking like it had been clenched in an angry fist.

I figured she hadn't learned the thing she needed to. The thing she offered me—it wasn't a thing I was interested in. Don't ever tame your demons, but keep them on a leash. Maybe I should have shared that, before she went full Tasmanian Devil on me. Control is better than ignorance.

I tried to push myself up and remembered after a brief bout

with screaming that my arm was still dislocated. I slid on my butt over to a doorframe and slammed my shoulder into it. Several more screams—I was starting to sound like one night with Yoko Ono—and a good bout of tears, and it was popped back in as far as it would go.

I glared at Anne's body. "What did you hope to accomplish?"

She didn't answer in the way that dead people don't. I stared at her a little longer, feeling like there should be a lesson here, some great epiphany, some great understanding. Instead, I just felt sad. The things people do for power—they break you. No one seeks to understand, just to own. Everything but their own shit, usually.

I stood on shaky legs and headed for the door, halting on the way out. I shuffled through her drawers until I found what I was looking for—a sheet of paper, filled with names, and beside each, an angelic circle. After a second of thought, I made my way back to the kitchen and turned up the oven, then limped my way out of the house. My knee was swollen, but I didn't think it busted. I was glad to put the smell of roast behind me. Besides, I had bigger problems. I knew what it was Ramirez wanted now, and what he'd been up to.

The problem was, how do you stop a war?

25

I called Ivy as soon as I managed to limp my way from the woman's house. She agreed to meet me outside the church. While I sat there, bruised and bleeding, I did a quick inventory of my decisions. Ivy was right. I was going to need a break soon. I hurt everywhere. What little good her potion had done me, I'd undone and thrown off like a kid that doesn't want to wear pants.

It didn't take long for her to pull up in the Beamer. She was wearing clean clothes and appeared freshly showered. I raised an eyebrow, and she shrugged. Then she got a good look at me and sighed in exasperation.

"What?" I asked.

"You know, I have finite funds."

"Which means?"

"It means if you keep acting like your body is a rental, you're going to be fucked at some point. I can only patch you up so much." She paused for a minute. "And I like having you around."

An awkward silence descended between us. I rubbed the back of my neck and looked across the plaza. Finally, I cleared my throat.

"Fair," I said. "I like being around."

"So, what's up?"

"I think I know what Ramirez and Cory are up to."

"Fill me in while we drive," she said.

I hopped in the car, and she pulled away from the curb.

"That circle was my first clue. Ramirez bound an angel to Cory. Maybe to himself."

"Why? How? Wouldn't that kill him?"

I shook my head. "I don't know. Apparently not. I think at the least, he's unhinged. As to the why—I think he got it in his head to cleanse the demons. What he's doing instead is starting a war."

"Why?"

"I don't think it was intentional. I think he bound that angel and realized too late they're aggressive assholes. You ever read the Bible? Like if Heaven had the internet and Michael was obsessed with being an alpha male. All he had to do was give them an in into the world, and they're ready to fight."

She grimaced. "Great."

"They didn't like it when we were made. Imagine being bound to one of us."

"Ick," she said.

"Same," I said.

"Did you find that other thing I asked you to look into?"

She nodded as we turned a corner. "Rumor is there's a witch working with them."

"Thought as much. That explains the bear fetish and the coin firestarter. You know anyone with a grudge?"

Her hands tightened on the wheel. "Not a grudge, per se, but we never did figure out what happened to the Ice Queen. I did a little digging. Her name's Caroline. Morally flexible, true mercenary. If she's involved, she thinks she can profit from it."

"You found her?"

"Yeah, my contacts saw her in Caesar's yesterday."

"She with anybody?"

"Not that they noticed."

I cursed. "We're gonna have to do this the old-fashioned way. You think you can lean on her?"

"Sure thing, Mugsy."

"What?"

"Lean on her? What are you, like a hundred?"

"Rough her up? Enhance some interrogation?"

She made a face at that but nodded. "Better. Still old, but better."

"I don't catch a lot of TV."

"God, you *are* old. Everybody streams these days."

"What the hell's that?"

"You know what? Just spend like, five minutes on the internet, Grandpa."

I muttered something about whippersnappers, and Ivy laughed. She pointed the Beamer downtown. I steeled myself for what was next.

W e pulled up in front of a Chinese restaurant with neon signs in the window and paper lanterns out front. I glanced in the window—they did a brisk business. Most of the seats were full, and more people were filing in.

"I *was* hungry," I said.

Ivy pointed up, at the row of apartments above the restaurant. I looked. Most had heavy curtains drawn. One was cracked, and a shadow moved behind them.

"She's renting a place up there."

"How you want to handle this?" I asked.

She looked at me and pursed her lips. "You stay down here."

"What?"

"Stay."

She started toward the stairs leading to the apartments.

"But…"

Ivy paused, looked back. "This is a witch thing. You want to mess with that?"

I did not. Still I didn't want her to get hurt. She must've read my mind because she snorted in annoyance and came back.

"Stay. Here."

"Ivy, we don—"

"Stay." She patted me on the head, and I watched her climb the stairs.

I could appreciate that much, at least. Fine, call me a sexist. I've got a lust demon under my skin. At least I wasn't humping the nearest telephone pole.

I alternated between watching the window and the stairs. Ivy still hadn't come down. I pushed off the car and took a step toward the door when a flash of light and a scream rebounded off the street. The patrons in the restaurant looked up, and I did the same in time to see the window blow out in a cloud of glass.

A body hurtled free, slamming into the building across the street, its impact crushing the brick façade. It fell to the street and groaned. Ivy appeared a moment later, stepping onto air like it was nothing. A corona of black fire surrounded her as she descended, her eyes pits of midnight.

She stepped across the street and picked Caroline up with one hand. I caught a glimpse of pale sallow skin and a ponytail. Ivy growled something I didn't understand, and the blonde screamed a word.

Finally, Ivy dropped her in a heap. The woman collapsed there, shaking and crying. The corona winked out from Ivy as she turned back to me, her eyes returning to normal.

"All yours," she said.

I raised an eyebrow but kept any comments I might've had to myself. There's a season for everything, and snark was definitely out for the moment. I walked over to the woman and crouched beside her. She didn't look hurt, but she sure acted it.

"Hey," I said. I tapped her forehead, and her eyes focused on me. She blanched, and I gave her a smile. "Yeah, it's me. You burnt my house down, jackhole. You also stuck a spike in my chest. Now you're going to tell me where your boss is."

She sputtered something, and I leaned in.

"What?" I asked.

She sputtered again, and a sudden gout of blood erupted from her throat. Her eyes rolled back, and she thrashed, drowning in her own blood. It was over in a moment. I sighed and stood.

"You a little rough with her?" I asked Ivy.

She shook her head, a frown creasing her face. "She did that herself. Secret-keeping curse. Wherever she knew, Ramirez *really* doesn't want it getting out."

We walked back to the car. The restaurant patrons were watching us, their meals forgotten. I took a bow, as if it was all an act. Ivy followed suit. Blank looks prevailed only a moment longer, then a smattering of applause came to us. I looked over at Ivy.

"We should probably leave."

As if on cue, sirens echoed through the streets. We hopped in the Beamer and sped away.

———

We'd made it back to Ivy's apartment without incident. I managed to get a shower and a whiskey in, and lay on the couch, staring at the ceiling, Ivy in the chair beside me.

"Now what?" She asked.

I shrugged.

"That's useful," she said.

"I am a font of usefulness." In truth, I felt like an aching tooth. Nearly every part of me hurt. "Did Caroline spit anything useful out before she karked it?"

"Just a name."

"Which was?"

"The Enclave."

I cursed. The old man was getting to be a real thorn in my side. I didn't know what we'd find when we visited that old mean group of bastards, but I hoped it wasn't a pile of bodies. Call me an optimist.

26

She pulled away from the curb, the Beamer accelerating smoothly. The car slid through traffic like shit through an angry chihuahua. No small feat, considering the time of day. The strip mall came into view, and Ivy slowed.

"Anyone ever tell you that you drive like Jeff Gordon on speed?"

"Bitch, I am Dale Earnhardt."

I did my best not to mention that Dale had died in a fiery crash. Sometimes not tempting fate is the best option.

The mall parking lot was empty, though that wasn't an indication of anything. The cigar shop windows were tinted, only the neon Open sign indicating they were still ready for business. Ivy maneuvered the Beamer into a spot by the door and killed the engine.

"You ready?" She asked.

I took a breath. I was about to tell three of the most powerful people in the city that my mentor had somehow flown under their radar, sacrificed a child, recruited another binder and a witch, and was planning on starting a war. In the realm of things that make me make a sound like a sick teakettle, that was pretty high up there.

Ivy joined me on the sidewalk.

"What're you waiting for?" She asked.

"My heart to stop trying to escape my ribs."

"What the worst that could happen?" She asked and pushed the door open.

I stopped in my tracks. Bodies hung from the industrial fans in the ceiling, spinning lazily. The cute bartender was among them, the tattoos on her arms still smoking. I crept up to the body. Her neck was bent at a downward angle, and I saw the blackball between her lips. Someone had burned the demons out of these people.

"This. This is pretty bad," I said.

"Uh-huh." Ivy reached into her bag and pulled out a thin willow branch.

"A wand?"

I pulled the pistol from inside my jacket, checked the slide.

"We've all got our phallic toys," she said.

We crept through the room. It smelled of ozone and copper and released bowels. Something hit me in the ear, and I ducked, bringing the pistol to bear. A man, his throat distended from the rope around it, swayed with the impact. I let out a breath. Ivy gave me a wry look, then nodded at the door on the far end.

If you've ever seen those films where the hero is creeping toward the cellar door, and the audience knows there's something down there, you have an idea of how I felt about this. Scared, nervous, a little annoyed. I flipped the safety off. Probably would've been useful earlier. I paused in front of the door.

Thing about powerful people getting their shit pushed in. Everyone talks about wanting to do it. No one really considers having to deal with the people who do. So, I took the easy way out.

I squared up with the door and unloaded the pistol.

The rune-tipped rounds tore through the hardwood, leaving smoking holes. The smells of cordite and woodsmoke filled the air, along with a slight haze. My ears rang, and I barely noticed the sound of brass hitting the floor. When it was over, silence settled on the room. Ivy cocked an eyebrow and looked at me, hand on hip.

"Little warning would've been nice."

"Yeah, for the guy on the other side. 'Ivy, I'ma shoot this door' is just a big red flag."

"It's also a courtesy."

I pushed the door open. Cory lay on the other side, clutching a wound in his leg. A pool of blood stained the floor. The Enclave hung here, too, their tattoos smoking. A broken blackball lay on the floor, the obsidian cracked. Cory had burned the demons out of these people as well. Likely before he'd killed them. I knelt beside my former lover, pressed the pistol against the hole in his leg, and tried not to think of how much power it had required to take down the three corpses in the room. If things were about to go bad, they were going to go very bad.

"Ivy," I said.

Cory froze. She knelt beside me and opened his shirt. A new circle had been tattooed on his chest. It was Enochian, but not the demonic dialect. The lines were orderly, clean. Almost obsessive. Leave it to angels to be anal retentive. I pressed the pistol into his wound, and he sucked in a breath, tried not to scream.

"Where's Ramirez?" I asked.

"Get fucked."

I sighed. "History doesn't matter to you?"

"Not since you took up with this… whore." Cory spat.

Ivy fetched him a blow aside his head. He winced.

"Ramirez," I said.

He snarled and pushed me back. The circle on his chest flared, and he was suddenly on his feet. He grabbed Ivy and whipped her against the wall. She cried out, and then I was calling on Regnos.

I launched myself at him, the pistol forgotten for the moment. It's really hard to interrogate someone with a smoking hole in their torso.

He backhanded me casually, sending me crashing into the fireplace. I groaned and rolled over, and he stepped to me, a rope in his hands.

"You were given every opportunity to quit," he said.

He looped the rope around my neck and started dragging me across the floor. The skin of my throat burned from the rough fibers, and I scrabbled at them with hands desperate to break free. Regnos' claws made purchase, and I began to saw at the fibers.

Cory paused, throwing one end of the rope around an exposed beam. He grabbed it and began to haul me up, rope around his shoulder as he set to work.

"You don't understand anything. When Ramirez came to me, he was grieving, broken. You had failed him so many times. And you were flawed. A criminal." He scoffed, and gravity helped to strangle me as I rose. I sawed faster.

"All he ever wanted was a son. More, all he ever wanted was peace. Peace for everyone with demons."

He tugged the rope and tied it off, turning his back. Regnos screamed, and I ripped the fraying rope from my neck. I fell, collapsing to the floor in a heap. Black stars swam in my vision, and I heaved fresh air into my lungs.

Cory spun and limped back to me. He grabbed me by the hair, and I unleashed Llyrial. His hand wavered.

"No," he said through gritted teeth. "Unclean."

I reached up and grabbed his stiffening cock, my demon battering him with waves of lust. He faltered again.

"Nnn," he grunted.

I made a fist and pushed Llyrial back, Regnos' strength taking the place of lust. Cory screamed in agony as I crushed a testicle. I bore him to the ground, still holding his genitals, and pinned his arms with my legs.

"Where. Is. Ramirez." I asked, punctuating each word with an increase in pressure.

"Under... under the church!" He wept.

I didn't have to ask which church. There were only so many demonite churches in the city, and Bill's would be out of commission for a while. That left the one on 4th. I let him go, and he curled into a fetal position, clutching his balls. He heaved once and vomited a steaming pool of bile onto the carpet.

"Too late," he whispered to himself.

"What?"

"Too late."

Then his head exploded, and blue light streamed from him, slipping toward the ceiling and through the ventilation system. I wondered if that would come back to bite me in the ass again, then decided I had enough on my plate already.

As relationship endings go, that's one Cosmo had never included.

Ivy stood from across the room, the tip of her wand glowing. She limped over to me and sat heavily. I wrapped an arm around her.

"Under the church?"

"Yep," I said.

"Shitshow?"

"Yep."

She shrugged. "Let's do this."

I nodded and picked up the pistol. At least I didn't have to worry about the Cleansing. I wondered what our friendly neighborhood cop would think of this. But first, I had to do something.

I looked at the tattoos on the Enclave bodies. Still smoking, but the runes were clear. While most were different, everything from lust to rage, all three bodies shared one—exact down to sigil and size. I inspected the language there and realized what they'd been keeping hidden.

"Get a knife," I said.

"Why?"

"I have an idea."

27

The new runes still itched. Ivy did the best she could with what she had, but you can only do so much with raw flesh. At least they'd stopped bleeding. I did my damndest to ignore the ache while I made a call to Detective Roberts. He went from incredulous to annoyed pretty quick. Regardless, I was willing to give him the benefit of the doubt. Worst case, he ignored me. Best case, he showed up in time to tag the corpses. I just hoped it wasn't the middle ground: shoot Jack on sight and sprinkle some crack on him.

I didn't know when the fires started, but as we drove through the streets, it was clear they were set to flush demonites out. People fought in the streets, some quick and brutal, others like a ballet. Part of me wanted to stop and lend a hand. Another realized I'd be as useful as nipples on a boar if I didn't cut off the source.

What bothered me more was that EMS were seemingly slow to respond. The fires and the casualties were going to mount if someone didn't intervene soon. I wondered how high the conspiracy went. Cops possessed by angels. Not shocking. Same chip on their shoulders, same small man, big gun attitude. I wondered how the detective was dealing with this after our call. I figured if he saw me right now, he'd be just as likely to shoot me as arrest me. There was that middle ground again. The only thing buoying my spirits was the knowledge I never do things in half-measures. He'd probably at least give me a beating, too.

Ivy skidded a corner as a gas line went up, blasting a house to flinders. Flaming scraps of *something* littered the ground. I hoped it was the contents of a deep freeze.

"Hey, uh, quick thing," I said.

"Yeah," Ivy said, slaloming around a knot of men with black eyes hammering into a group of people with blazing wings.

"I've got to kind of… wink out for a few."

"Wink out? You're gonna take a fucking nap?"

"Trust me, that's preferable. But we need all the help we can get. There's no way Ramirez doesn't have goons. And God only knows how many angels he's bound to himself."

"Fuck."

I nodded.

"How long?" She accelerated through a red light, narrowly missing a city bus.

I didn't know which was worse—being conscious during her driving or confronting the new demon.

I shrugged.

"Did you just shrug?"

"Yes."

"Fuck. Well, get to it. I am not fighting a fucking angel and his damn frat bros."

I closed my eyes and tried to visualize the Maze. I felt reality go wobbly, and the bottom of the world fall out.

I found myself under a stone arch on an obsidian island, words carved into the keystone.

"There is no final curtain, this is not a stage,
Can you read what's written on this blackened page?"

Cute. Very goth. Much brooding.

Through the gate, I saw three identical arches, each straddling the road at equal intervals, the last at the entrance to the obelisk itself, and again, starting at each of the spokes and then outward, ending at what I guessed to be eight identical gates at the end of each street.

I stepped forward, and the earth fell away. I floated in the blackness for a moment, and then—wings—I had not had them for millennia. No, the demon hadn't. I was just Jack.

Someone was speaking.

"...failure..."

I knelt, head bowed. The hall and floor were marble, though stained, and chipped, scorched in places. The roof was open to the sky.

"Legion."

I did not raise my head.

———

We had laid siege to the Throne for nine days—nine days of blood and fire and steel, and our host had nearly gained the upper hand. On the ninth, we saw a rout, our forces beaten, thrown from their entrenchments and scattered to the winds. I watched as the ones who had been unfortunate enough to be captured were impaled. Their immortal bodies turned eternally on spikes of pearl and ebony, blood flowing freely, forming rivers of red. The rest of us, the few who were deemed worthy, were placed on trial, a tribunal of One holding council.

"..sentence you to Exile." He had stopped speaking.

I listened for more, but none came—judgment was utter and final. The hall echoed in complete silence for a fraction of a second, the void terrible, then erupted in a cacophony of sound, like hammers in a windstorm.

The hair on my body stood on end, and then, erupted into flame as I was stripped, Divinity ripped from me, wings shorn from my back, and blood erupting from the wounds until I thought the world would snuff itself in blackness.

All around, the wind became a hurricane, the hammers steel plates crashing like cymbals from a Wagnerian opera. The ground fell away, and I was falling, down, down...

———

I was through the gate and on my knees, sucking air in great whooping gasps, and fighting the daisies blooming behind my eyes from the pain. Then it was gone, and I was on my feet again. Ahead, the second gate, and the third, and so on. I was already not looking forward to this in any way, due to what I could only describe as an utter goddamn lack of fun.

———

I stood at the entrance to the second gate, looking through it to the city beyond.

That's not what's really through there, is it? *I thought.* No, because that would be easy and easy doesn't make Jack cry.

"Fuck it." *I said to no one in particular and stepped through.*

Again, the blackness, a feeling of the ground dropping away, of being relocated. Then it was gone, and I was in bed, silk sheets covering naked skin. An ashtray sat beside me on a night table, the touch lamp set to its lowest setting, and casting the room in a moon-like glow.

I smelled incense—roses and myrrh—and felt the body beside me contract, then stretch in sleep. Her feet touched my leg, her calves brushing mine, and my skin erupted in gooseflesh as she pushed back, *her bottom resting on my hip, her hair on my shoulder. She smelled fresh, clean.*

I ran a finger from thigh to shoulder and watched her shiver—that had always tickled her. I rolled to spoon her, and my hands found her chest, fingers tracing collar and breastbones, over ribs and up again to her breasts, her nipples hardening under my touch. She moaned, and pushed into me, and my lips were on the nape of her neck, and I was inside her.

Darkness again, and we were on cold grass, trees all around us, stretching baring limbs to the sky. She was arched like a cat, fingers and knees and toes dug into the mud between the blades of the clearing, and we hammered together, wet and bare, cries startling the birds.

Once more darkness, and we were in an alley, her body backed up to cold stone, steam from grates rising around us. One leg around my waist, skirt at her hips while I entered her, my hand at her throat, her hair in dirty strings around her face and eyes. She bared her teeth and bit my shoulder while I rammed her against the wall. She didn't love me, she said.

Fair enough.

———

T*he gate was gone, and I was on an empty street, this part of the town bare—no buildings, no trees, only sere brown grass and wind moaning as it followed the curve. Ahead, the next arch.*

———

A*nother alley, this one filled with ash and smoke. Rome was burning, had done so for six days, in a fire so intense it had blackened the stones of the walkways, scorched the buildings and weakened their foundations. I placed my hand on a wall and uttered a Word, watching the stone shatter, then erupt into flame.*

I walked into a main causeway, and someone—it looked like a

Legionnaire, tried to stop me. I shattered his bones, caused his heart to explode in his chest, and his eyes to melt from their sockets. Fuck him.

Nero had betrayed me, and this was his payment. I stepped over the burning corpses of men and women, children still wrapped in swaddling clothes, and with another Word, set the whole of the hills ablaze.

———

I was in the center of the city, the obelisk rising above me. It was made of ebony and obsidian, the stones merged in a way that were seamless, black swirling into black. I leaned against it and slid to the ground, unsure about the next flood of memories, the next betrayal by things I had thought long dead. I closed my eyes and heard voices.

"...so I said, why don't you?"

"Bring this to Titus. He'll need to see the reports from the..."

"He's dead? What happened to..."

I opened my eyes and saw the city, the plaza filled with the dead, their ghosts lingering in pale black and white, flickering in and out of existence like an old film reel. For a moment I wondered why they had stopped talking, why I could only hear bits and pieces of conversation, and I realized it was because they were looking at me.

They stared with wide, empty eyes, as though they themselves had seen a ghost. One of them pointed, its jaw opening and stretching, falling wide like a door off its hinges, a high, keening wail issuing from its maw. The sound was like nails on a chalkboard, amplified to the pitch of a jet engine, and I clamped my hands over my ears as the others began to join in, the scene resembling a tribunal.

I gained my feet and ran for the next gate, not caring anymore what the next picture it would show me was, as long as it meant escape from that unearthly jury. They cornered me, and at every turn, horror. Cold hands gripped my wrists, angry and pleading at the same time.

"Jack," they said in a chorus of cold voices. "Retribution. Peace will come after."

Then they were rushing, running, flying, floating, and I felt them, *their chill, entering me, one after the other, violating me, filling my soul, and pushing me to the side. It went on for what felt like forever, the pain growing in agonizing waves, until it felt the blood in my veins would freeze, and my retina would ice over.*

As each entered, I was flooded with a different set of memories—marriages and murders, love and sex and death and sacrifice, all until I thought I would go mad. I fought, chained them with will, named them as they had been named once before.

"Legion."

———

I came to the surface, gasping for air. The car had stopped, Ivy leaning over with a concerned look on her face. She breathed a sigh of relief.

"Oh, thank fuck. You're not dead."

"Sorry, waking up a demon the hard way. Wait. Did I seem dead?"

"You seemed not alive."

"Is that... is that not the same?"

"It's not different."

"I'm confused."

"Me too. Come on," she nodded toward the church through the window. "We're there."

28

I t was quiet outside the church. I didn't want to say too quiet, but it was enough to make me check my pistol. It almost felt like cheating. But that was the one nice thing about guns. They *were* cheating. Sure, you can make arguments for feeding your family, for self-defense, for competition shooting. But at the end of the day, they existed for one reason: to make as big a hole as possible in something living.

A high wall surrounded the grounds, the rectory tucked on the opposite end of the yard. Nothing much had changed since the last time I'd been here. Still, it felt off, and I knew better than to ignore my gut. I looked up, past the recently shingled roof, to the bell tower. Ivy glanced over at me.

"Not thinking about going on a shooting spree?"

"No..."

"Well, what then?"

"Well, Cory said Ramirez was in the basement."

"Under the church, technically."

"Thank you, Captain Pedantic. Anyway, if I were an angel trapped in a man's body, I'd want to get as high as possible."

"You think he's in the steeple."

"I think Cory spent a lot of time lying to both of us."

"Good point. Let's go."

She kicked the gate open. It hammered into the fence, sending a clatter and clang through the courtyard. I glared at her.

"Why?" I asked.

A roar went up from across the yard, a mass of bodies pouring from the church. They didn't look like they wanted to dance.

"Ah," I said.

I pulled the pistol. It was easy to shoot Cory. He was an asshole. And the Word wasn't an option. It might be the power of creation, or fragments of it, but to mortals, it might as well be an industrial blender. These people—I didn't know how many Ramirez had bound against their will, and I wasn't willing to scatter their limbs like chaff. I glanced over at Ivy.

"Nonlethal," I said, holstering the gun.

"Boy, you must be out of your damn mind."

Still, she dumped the wand back in her bag and pulled a pestle and mortar free.

"What's that do?"

"This."

She stepped forward and ground the pestle against the stone bowl. A low-pitched rumble echoed through the air, and the mass of enraged angelus stumbled, then threw their hands over their ears. She ground harder, and I heard demonspeak in the notes. The angelus screamed, and began to collapse, only a few defying the sound.

I stepped in front of her and snapped off a couple haymakers as a line of stragglers tried to crowd us, Regnos raging beneath the surface. The demon was ready for a little violence, and each blow was hard and fast, knocking the possessed out of the fight.

One got through, and it screamed a word in Enochian, the ground around me rattling and erupting in stone spikes. I leapt back in time to avoid being a Jack-kebab, though several still managed to rip holes in my jacket and leave a dozen bloody scores across my flesh.

Ivy retaliated in kind, a word of magic peeling the flesh from the man like the rind from an orange. He staggered, then started to scream. I put a bullet in his skull to make it stop. It's one thing to want to save lives. It's another to prolong their suffering.

A second came at her from behind a low row of hedges, a skinny brunette wearing a pencil skirt and a Hello Kitty shirt. Ivy spun on the woman, reaching out with her hand bent like a claw. She pressed her fingers into the woman's chest and snapped her arm back like a whip. Something glowing and soft blue clung to her palm. I shuddered.

The body collapsed, and Ivy tossed the woman's soul away like stray trash.

I took a breather, hands on my knees. Ivy shot a smirk at me.

"Out of shape?"

"Little bit," I gasped.

A keening wail went up, and the doors of the nearby rectory opened, disgorging a horde of men and women armed with kitchen implements and gardening tools. Each unfurled blazing wings. I groaned in frustration. At this rate, we were going to be trampled into the dirt before we even reached the church.

The sound of a screaming diesel engine cut through the din, and I turned to see a massive black semi, scarred with a score of claw marks, tearing toward the courtyard fence. It hopped the curb, and I yanked Ivy out of the way as it ripped across the yard's grass. It belched black smoke, then slammed into the crowd of rabid angel-possessed, scattering them like bowling pins.

The truck ground to a halt in the sudden silence, and Roberts staggered from the cab. He plopped on the grass and lit a cigarette.

I hurried over. He was disheveled, and one eye was a swollen purple egg. "You okay?" I asked.

"No," he said around his cigarette, "Had to fight a trucker after my squad car got busted up. I'm hurt. I'm pissed. Probably gonna need a new job. Oh, and an angel ate my sergeant's face."

"Ah, that's a shame."

"Not really. He was a dick."

"Ah." I chalked the callousness up to shock.

Roberts squinted up at me. "Don't you have a job to do?"

I nodded and rejoined Ivy. The survivors, about twenty men and women, lay on the ground, slumbering peacefully. We picked our way through them and to the church. I paused at the door to tie my shoe, which had somehow become undone in the chaos.

"You're bad at English," I said.

"The fuck you talkin' about?"

"*Non*lethal. As in no deading people."

"Hey, most of them are still alive. No thanks to the cop."

"Yeah, but that lady you ripped the soul from is definitely dead."

"Picky, for a guy who just had his life saved."

"Way I see it, beggars can be choosers. Why eat shit when you can eat leftover tuna?"

I finished tying my shoe. Ivy squinted at me.

"You done?" She asked.

She held a thick rod in one hand, carved from willow, and a bowl in the other. Another item from her bag. I straightened and took in the church one more time.

"No one ever appreciates my philosophy," I said.

"That's because your philosophy sounds suspiciously like bullshit."

"I'm a prophet."

"Let's go, you cut-rate Deepak Chopra."

We paused for a moment, neither of us meaning the words we said. It was just a way to keep the shadow off our souls, fear from the door. We stepped to the entrance.

"Last chance to turn around," I said.

"You first."

I summoned Regnos and kicked in the door. Strength flooded me, and the jamb splintered, the door flying free and smashing into the wall, sending echoes across the pews within. I rushed in, ready for any scene. Except the one I saw.

Whatever was going on here, the hint of madness the plaster Jesus had shown had turned to true insanity. I blamed whatever plan Ramirez had put into place. The statue had ripped itself free from the cross and was busy devouring Cory's spirit. I saw him as a bright blue outline tapering to a point. It would have been comical, if not for the look on the god's face, one of utter rage and hunger. Cory screamed, then noticed me, and started pleading.

"Jesus Christ! Help me! Help me, motherfucker! I take back all the bad shit! I promise I'll leave you alone, just helAAAAa-AaARGBLE"

His words cut off as the statue sucked him in like an errant strand of spaghetti. It turned toward Ivy and I, eyes blazing blue with devoured spirits. Hard way to watch someone go. I swallowed, hard, and charged, Regnos still holding my brain in thrall. My fist lashed out, slamming into what would have been hamstring. Instead, chunks of plaster flew, dust puffing into the air. Unconvinced, the statue continued toward Ivy.

She shouted and thrust the rod into the bowl she still held, and for the first time I noticed it was filled with something bright and clear. It splashed and coated the rod, and she flicked it at the statue. Metallic drops spattered its front and sizzled, eating through the paint and plaster. Still, it advanced, and a hand at the end of an over-muscled arm snatched her by the throat, lifting her.

Ivy made a strangled choking sound, and I pulled the talisman she'd given me from my pocket, clenching it in my fist. I rushed forward, pulling on more of Regnos.

The edges of my vision went dim. The world flickered. And

then my fist punched through the statue, shattering its center to pieces. With a sighing groan, it crumbled apart, plaster caking the floor. Ivy sucked in deep breaths and rubbed her throat. I tried not to think about having seen my former lover die twice in the same day.

"Jesus. I am so going to have to say like a thousand Hail Mary's for that one," I said between gasps of air.

We caught our breath for a moment, then made our way to the back of the nave, where a curtained apse hid a flight of stairs. We started up. The steps were wooden and creaked with our passage.

"At least he'll know we're coming," I said.

"The only way he couldn't know is if he was in Ohio, Jack. And then he'd be mad he was in Ohio."

"What've you got against Ohio?"

She shrugged. "Isn't being Ohio enough? How about it looks like a greeting trapped between two holes."

"You should write Hallmark cards. Happy Birthday, sorry you're trapped in Sphincterville."

We hit the halfway point. I looked down. It was a long way down. Far enough down that if either of us fell, we'd pop like a bag full of pudding. Ivy came to stand beside me.

"Whatcha thinking about?" She asked.

"Pudding."

"Butterscotch?"

"Sure, butterscotch. *Not* entrail."

"What?"

"What?"

We started climbing again. About two-thirds of the way up, Ivy broke the silence again.

"You ever seen a John Carpenter movie?" She asked.

I peeked over the side. The long drop was even longer. I looked back up and kept going.

"Can't say I have."

"Shame. Anyway, he made a lot of movies about social issues couched in horror tropes."

"Yeah, this remind you of one?"

"Big Trouble in Little China. Or maybe They Live. But only because you keep getting the snot kicked out of you."

"Thanks."

"Hey, it's your face. It inspires something in people. Anyway, the hero is always this working-class guy who keeps coming up against impossible odds and bulling through no matter what."

"Yeah? Am I the plucky hero in this situation?"

"You should know it doesn't always end well for that guy."

"You're a beam of sunshine," I said.

We cleared the head of the stairs, coming out into the belfry. Ramirez leaned against the wall, the open arch behind him commanding a view of the city. His arms were crossed over his chest, his eyes still pools of ink. The stairs rumbled and creaked behind us, and I spun in time to see Praedolor tearing up the flight. Ivy squared off with the demon. I turned back to Ramirez. He pushed off the wall and took a step forward, tilting his head until his vertebrae cracked.

My guts squirmed. I hadn't seen the man in ages, and I had a lot of feelings. Take one part abandonment issues, two parts abusive family, add a dash of bitterness, two shakes of betrayal, and an urge to punch someone in the head, and you get the idea of the cocktail that was brewing. I like to call it Fuck You, Pops.

"Mijo. Welcome home," he said.

29

"Old man." I nodded at him, and quietly called on Regnos. Or tried to. Ramirez did something, made some gesture, and the demon retreated with a whimper. I reached for Llyrial and Xiphos, and each gave no indication they had heard. I felt the skin on my hands smooth and didn't like the implication. I didn't like a lot of things at that moment. Not the memories, not the feelings jumbled up in my gut and doing their best to make me vomit on someone's Volvo a few hundred feet below.

"You get what you wanted?" I asked. "Killed that girl and her father for your little cause."

"You don't get it."

"What don't I get? What's so important you'd sacrifice a human life? I don't know who you are, but you're certainly not the man I knew."

"No, I'm not. That man is dead."

"So that's three you killed," I said, making a circle. Ramirez flexed his hands. I knew that tell. He was about to strike. I had to keep him talking. "Tell me then. What's worth a life? Teach me."

"No. No more. You're a lost cause. You and all the others. You always did learn the hard way," he said, and launched himself at me.

I sidestepped his lunge, putting the tower's bell between us. "Wait. I haven't even heard your monologue."

Ramirez stepped around the bell; his pace measured. I pushed down another flood of emotion and memory threatening to soften my response. *Summer days in the barn, the smell of hay in the loft. Beers at dusk on the porch.* He held his hands wide.

"You want to know why, no?"

"Sure," I said, skirting the bell.

"Tainted. Unclean. Diseased. Evil. Those are the words they use for us. And do you know why?"

"Because we like peanut butter potato chip sandwiches?"

He snarled. "Because the demons use us, and not the other way around. They want what they've always wanted. Our souls. Our lives. They ruin us, and everything they touch. And you— you *cradle* them," he spat. "Filth."

Blazing wings erupted from his back, and he launched himself across the tower. I slipped to the side, putting the bell between us and gave it a shove. It slammed into him with a clang, and I heard a muttered curse. Behind me, heat blossomed as Ivy launched an attack at the demon. It screamed in rage, and she screamed back.

I crept around the bell. Ramirez was nowhere to be seen. I turned to Ivy. Praedolor was keeping its distance, pacing the boards of the tower, claws clicking. The sound sent shivers up my back, and I wondered if he wasn't right. If what we harbored was horror. I shook it off. No time for distraction.

"Where the hell is he?" I asked.

She shrugged, and Praedolor lunged. Ivy backpedaled, sending a purple lash of energy into its nose. It whimpered and I gave a little cheer.

Something heavy and angry slammed into me from behind, bearing me down. I'd forgotten the bastard could fly. Ramirez had swooped through the open arch. If he wasn't beating my skull against the floorboards, I might even be impressed. Instead, my brain was screaming in pain, I tasted blood, and my vision flickered.

I'm twenty-five, just out of prison. I can barely stand the open spaces, the crush of humanity. I jump when someone touches my shoulder, nearly braining them with a fist. Then Ramirez comes along. We meet at my day job, me swinging a hammer from nine to five, in this case building a deck for him. Simple work, keeps my hands and my head busy.

The sun goes down, and we're packing up our tools. The old man and I get to talking. Says he sees himself in me. I think it's a come-on. But free beer is free beer. We sit and talk, and he tells me about the demons.

SLAM. My head bounced off the chapel boards.

I'm 30 and standing over the old man's body. Weeping til I can't breathe. This is what it's like to lose a parent. A real parent. Not the things I'd been saddled with. A gap in my life now, where before there had been compassion and patience and understanding. My heart feels like it's tearing in two.

Praedolor screamed in pain, snapping me from the memory. The demon flew through the air, tearing Ramirez off me. I rolled onto my back and pulled the pistol, sighting down the barrel as my former mentor found his feet. I had to blink the tears away.

Too slow. The demon found its feet and kicked the gun from my hands. I watched it sail through the arch Ramirez had flown through and into the wild yonder.

"Fuck," I muttered.

Ivy blasted Praedolor with another lance of fire, this one tight and thin. It tore through the demon, and it staggered back. Ramirez took the opening the distraction provided and leapt, legs pinning me to the ground. His hands closed around my throat and began to squeeze.

"Forty years," he panted. "Forty years in the service of evil.

And then one day, Cory comes to me, and I see someone who's been hurt by our *gifts*. You were shit to him, Jack."

To punctuate this, he slammed my head against the floorboards.

Summer sun, my hands and feet trying to coordinate the clutch and the shifter, and Ramirez with infinite patience.

SLAM.

Winter, and snow heavy at the Rest. A fire in the hearth, and us curled up in overstuffed chairs, books on our laps.

SLAM.

His fists raining down in a flurry as we train. Every strike precise, calculated. Enough to hurt, not enough to bleed. Lessons there, too.

Why is it every lesson I learn is written in pain? Why is it the people I love prefer agony to compassion? Is it a fundamental flaw with me? Some questions you can never know the answers to. Some questions leave a black mark on your heart and soul. You learn to live with it, or it eats you alive. I felt my world narrow, heard a tide of voices.

His hands loosened for a moment, and I sucked a breath in. Compassion? Or sadism? I found I didn't much care, as long as I could breathe, even if it felt like someone had poured fire down my throat. The black at the edge of my vision faded, though the voices didn't.

"Forty. Fucking. Years," he said.

"And for five of those, I loved you," I choked out.

Pain flooded my limbs as he rammed blazing claws into my shoulders, pinning me to boards. The world winked out for a moment.

Our mother screamed. It wasn't the first time, but this was louder than the others, different somehow. I heard fear in it, a terrible loneliness that comes from knowing the end is near. My stomach flipped, and I woke Ellie.

"Whazzit?" she asked, voice slurred by speech.

"Mom—Dad."

Ellie rolled over. "It's the same. Same as every night. Put a pillow over your head." Saying so, she pulled hers over her ears, and was snoring in no time.

I couldn't. Something about that sound had crept into my bones, and my heart quailed. I waited until I was sure Lucas was asleep and crept to the door. I eased it open and snuck into the hall, closing it silently behind me. I stood there for a moment, listening. The house was quiet, but for an odd chuffing sound. I thought I smelled copper. That hot scent you get in the basement, when the water's running. Anger rose in me. How could he do this? How could he be so brutal, such an animal? How did God let this happen?

My rage high in my throat, I crept to my parents' room at the end of the hall, and snuck in. After a moment of rummaging around in their closet, I came away with my father's pistol and a box of ammunition. I loaded the cylinder, and emboldened, made my way downstairs.

The gun was heavy. Part of me felt like I was wearing a sign screaming here I am *now, and another part worried that if my father caught me with the gun, he would give me the thrashing of a lifetime. I clutched it tighter and made my way through a dark living room, my feet taking me to the kitchen, my mother's sanctuary. Her favorite place.*

The copper smell was stronger here and was mixed with the odors of shit and urine. I rounded the corner and stopped, heart in my throat, pounding like a parasite threatening to break free. My father was seated at the kitchen table, his head in his hands. Fat tears rolled off his nose and plopped to the wood of the table like rain. His hands were red, and it was smeared across his forehead and cheeks. The knife on the table glistened. My mother's knife. The one she used to cut bread and vegetables. Horror rose in me, competing with the rage.

I looked down, and saw my mother, eyes open, her stomach a red ruin. She had pressed her hands to the wound, and they were red to the wrists. Blood pooled around the body like an oil slick from a leaking tractor. I looked back to my father, the rage reaching a crescendo. I raised the pistol.

Finally, he noticed me, and turned red-rimmed eyes on me. He said nothing, and I did not offer. I pulled the trigger.

I came up full of rage and sorrow and called on my new passenger. Legion roared, and I felt the strength of a thousand demons infuse me. Their voices rose to a raging babble. I leashed my will and forced the cacophonous tide of personalities back. Ramirez's thumbs sought my windpipe, my vision spotting again.

I raised my hands as if to fight him off, then instead, dug into my jacket. The blackball was still there. I grabbed it, fingers closing over the slick cold surface. My throat ached. If this was what hanging felt like, I wanted none of it.

"No. More," Ramirez said.

I slammed the blackball into his teeth. Two split from his gums, and the sphere lodged in his mouth. He fell back, scrabbling at the obsidian, and I sucked in great lungfuls of air into my burning throat.

"We can at least agree on that," I said.

I spoke the Word. The blackball flared with a dark and terrible light. I felt the pull of gravity double, treble, and Ramirez screamed, a choked pitiful thing. His tattoos ignited, and he fell back, his eyes smoking. Something wailed, high and long, and then it was over. His body collapsed, a shell of flesh. I knelt and picked up the blackball, fighting back tears.

"Jack!" Ivy shouted.

Praedolor advanced on her, enraged.

"Fastball!" I said.

I threw the still-smoking sphere, and she hit it with a conjured blast of force. The obsidian slammed into the demon. For a moment, nothing happened, then Praedolor imploded, the stone shattering inward, sucking itself into a hole in reality.

When it was over, silence settled over the belfry. I lowered myself heavily to the floorboards. I'd seen and done a lot of fucked up things in my life. The worst of which wasn't even killing my former mentor and my ex. Still, you can't escape the punch in the gut that comes after, the shake, the tremor. It's a hell of a thing, killing a man. You take away all he's got and all he's ever gonna have. At least if you beat them, they can always get back up. But for few exceptions, I'd yet to see someone dig themselves from a grave.

Ivy sat beside me and wrapped an arm around me. I leaned my head on her shoulder and let the tears come, my heart heavy. Of all the things this had brought on, the worst of it was the loss of the girl and her father. I cursed myself for my stupidity, for not seeing the clues sooner.

Ivy leaned in and kissed me on the forehead, wiping away a spot of blood.

"We won, huh?"

It didn't feel like it, but I wasn't about to let her know. Not yet. You don't tug on Superman's cape, and you don't yuck someone's yum.

I wiggled a finger in my ear. "Yeah, I could go for wontons."

She leaned into me. "You're an idiot."

"I'm your idiot."

"And I'm your huckleberry."

"What?"

"Tombstone? Doc Holiday?"

I gave her a blank look.

"Seriously, I have a whole shelf of movies."

Something occurred to me and I cursed.

"Sorry," she said. "More of a book person?"

I shook my head. "I just realized something."

"What's that?"

"I am never going to get paid for this."

I lay back and stared up at the blue sky. Ivy lay beside me, her hand finding mine.

You probably think this is the end of things. But that's the thing about life and stories. They're a piece of the whole. We still had a group of asshole angels down in the courtyard. I had a busted-up Jesus and a smoking corpse in the church. There was a beat-up cop who was probably going to lose his job, *at best,* chain-smoking on the lawn. Somewhere out there, demons were still fighting angels, and sirens were more numerous than most busy Saturday nights in the city. But for the now, we had each other.

There aren't many wins in life. I think I'd already made my feelings on that clear. Hell, life has a way of turning even those pyrrhic. But I'd stopped a war. We'd saved... well, not a lot of lives, but enough. I was going to have to sort this out eventually. I owed the fence a favor. I was pretty sure I'd lost my personal demons and gained a whole crowd of them. My mentor, and two former lovers were dead. And my apartment was a smoking ruin.

Pyrrhus was probably a little jealous at this point. I wondered if they'd rename it a Nyxian Victory. I decided that maybe being historically famous was less a blessing and more a curse.

But all of these things were things that could wait til later. For now, it was enough to have Ivy and a few minutes' peace.

"You know what sounds good?" I asked.

"Wontons?"

"A vacation."

She rolled and rested her head on my chest. My own head rang like it was a tin duck in a shooting gallery. I turned and kissed her, full on the lips, my free arm pulling her into an embrace. I wasn't about to let the best thing that ever happened to me go for a while.

Better safe than sorry, and all that shit.

No, that's not right. Better safe than sorry implies you'll never take a risk. And I knew me well enough to know when I was lying to myself. I'd still take risks. Because that's what life is, right? Risk and reward.

"What's on your mind, Jack?" Ivy asked.

"I was thinking about how you never saw Bozo the Clown and Captain Kangaroo in the same room."

"What?"

"It's eerie. And what exactly was he Captain of? Captain of the Kangaroos? Have they organized? Are they a threat? Someone should do something."

"Shut up, Jack."

I shut up, and she gave me a squeeze. Sometimes a man has to know his limitations.

ACKNOWLEDGMENTS

I want to thank the usual suspects:
Angela
Krystle
Luke
Dave
Nick
Justine
Tom
Tom
Phil
You know who you are. Thank you for kicking my ass in the same way Jack gets his own beat. The book's better for it.

Printed in Great Britain
by Amazon

17653981R00129